A Dolphin Wish

Other books by Natalie Grant

Glimmer Girls series
London Art Chase (Book One)

faithgirlz

A Dolphin Wish

by Natalie Grant
with Naomi Kinsman

ZONDERkidz™

ZONDERKIDZ

A Dolphin Wish
Copyright © 2016 by Natalie Grant
Illustrations © 2016 by Cathi Mingus

This title is also available as a Zondervan ebook.

Requests for information should be addressed to:
Zonderkidz, 3900 Sparks Drive, Grand Rapids, Michigan 49546

ISBN 978-0-310-75253-0

Art direction: Cindy Davis
Cover design and interior illustrations: Cathi Mingus
Content contributor: Naomi Kinsman
Interior design: Denise Froehlich

Printed in the United States of America

17 18 19 20 21 22 /DCI/ 20 19 18 17 16 15 14 13 12 11 10 9 8 7 6 5

To my glimmer girls—Gracie, Bella, and Sadie.
You're my greatest adventure. I love you.

ACKNOWLEDGMENTS

Thank you to Naomi Kinsman for bringing your genius creativity and beautiful patience to this process. None of this would be a reality without you.

ONE

Mia was first into the beach bungalow, her sisters right behind her. They'd flown from London to San Diego to relax for a couple days before Mom's next concert. In London, they'd stayed in the over-the-top, amazing Musician's Penthouse, because the tour organizers had a special connection with the hotel. Their resort in San Diego was a collection of bungalows along the beach. Even though this bungalow was half the size of the London suite, to Mia, it was even better. For one thing, it opened right up onto the beach.

"Come on!" Maddie slid open the screen door, kicked off her shoes, and ran out onto the sand.

"Wait up!" Lulu shouted, dropping her suitcase in the middle of the floor.

Mia thought about picking up her sisters' suitcases. In the end, she dropped hers on the pile and raced after them. Lulu was fast for a six-year-old—a good thing, because she always wanted to race and hated losing. Maddie was fast too, but she was more of a dancer than a runner. Mia charged into the waves just behind Lulu, kicking up salt water and splashing her sister's legs. Lulu shrieked and splashed back. Maddie stayed at the edge of the water, leaping out of reach of each breaking wave.

When people first met the Glimmer family, it took a while for them to realize Mia and Maddie were twins. Mia was three inches taller and usually three steps in front, trying things out to make way for her sister. Still, no matter how many differences they had—or maybe because of their differences—Maddie was Mia's best friend in the whole world. Most of the time, Mia felt as though she could read Maddie's mind. Right now, unfortunately, not so much.

A blast of cold water in the face brought Mia out of her thoughts. "Wha . . . ?" Lulu howled with laughter, darting away before Mia could splash her back.

"You better run!" Mia said, laughing as she wiped the salt water off her cheeks.

Mia and Lulu splashed up and down the beach, tossing handfuls of water at Maddie every time they passed by her. She'd jump back, most of the time staying well out of the way.

"Girls!" Miss Julia jogged across the sand, her floppy hat threatening to blow off any second. "Sunscreen!"

Miss Julia lathered sunscreen on the girls' necks and the tips of their ears. Twice during the operation, Miss Julia's hat blew off her head and skittered across the sand. Both times, the girls helped her chase it down before it blew out to sea.

"Good grief," Miss Julia said, coming back to rub the last white marks into Lulu's shoulders.

Finally free, Lulu flung her arms wide and fell backward into the soft sand. "Cover me up! Cover me up!"

A Dolphin Wish

Mia's knees sunk into the sunbaked sand. When she scooped up a handful, it felt like holding grains of sunlight in her hands. Deeper down, the sand was cooler. Handful after handful, Mia and Maddie piled sand on top of their little sister's legs. Lulu squirmed and giggled. Soon, all they could see were her toes, her shoulders, and her face.

Lulu grinned a smile that no one could resist and said, "Pack it down! Make it into a sand blanket."

"Who is this sand creature?" Mom asked.

Mia looked up to see Mom and Dad smiling down at them. "Grraumb!" Lulu growled, playing along.

"Watch out!" Dad said. "I think she might be dangerous." Miss Julia snapped a picture of Lulu, the sand creature.

"Are you starting a new travelogue?" Lulu asked. "Can I help?"

"Yes, and yes!" Miss Julia said, holding the picture out for Lulu to inspect. "I need a sand monster face." Lulu scrunched her nose and growled again.

Mom laughed and laced her fingers through Dad's as Miss Julia took a second picture. "Better," Lulu decided, after checking the picture out.

Mom and Dad went to try out the beach chairs, and Maddie poked the sand above Lulu's belly button. "Can you feel this?"

"Nope!" Lulu said.

"How about this?" Maddie asked, drumming a beat on Lulu's knees.

11

"Not that either!" Lulu crowed.

Mia sat back on her heels, part of the game but also on the fringes of it. She almost felt as though she were watching her sisters through binoculars. Or maybe it was only Maddie who seemed farther away than usual. Ever since Maddie had snuck out of their hotel in London and chased down a thief—a completely un-Maddie-like thing to do—Mia felt like the world had turned upside down. It was the strangest feeling, as though someone had swapped her sister for a stranger.

"My turn!" Maddie said, flopping onto her back on the sand.

Lulu wriggled free and started piling sand on Maddie. "Come on, Mia. Help me!"

Maddie kept moving, so it was hard to cover her up, but after a few attempts they managed it. As soon as Mia and Lulu started patting the sand down, Maddie burst free.

She caught Mia's eye. "Your turn?"

"Maybe later," Mia said.

"Are you sure, Mia?" Mom called. "Because if you girls are done, I want you to rinse off, and then we'll go find something for dinner."

"Yay, dinner!" Lulu said. "I'm starved."

"Me too," Dad said.

"Come on, girls," Miss Julia said. "I'll help you get dressed."

TWO

Just down the beach from the hotel was a restaurant, close enough that the Glimmer family could walk. Mia took off her flip-flops and pressed her toes into the still-warm sand. The sun hadn't set yet, but the heat of the day had cooled. The tide was coming in—with each wave, the beach seemed to shrink further and further still.

"Tiki torches!" Lulu said, pointing ahead.

Sure enough, flames atop tiki torches flickered, lighting the way to the restaurant. Mia wasn't sure of the exact definition of a cabana, but *cabana* was the word that came to mind. The restaurant had a sea grass roof, a tiled floor dusted with fine sand, and wide open walls to let in the sea breeze. The waitstaff wore Hawaiian shirts, and a musician playing a ukulele wandered from table to table. Mia slipped her feet back into her flip-flops as a woman walked over to the sand-strewn entrance to greet them.

"Welcome. Choose any table you like," she said, gesturing to the half-filled restaurant. "Mid-week tends to be quiet."

Dad chose a table close to the beach. Mia chose the seat closest to the sand. After she sat, she realized Lulu or Maddie might have wanted this chair. But Maddie and

13

Lulu were deep in conversation, planning a sandcastle to build tomorrow, complete with three levels and a moat. They hardly noticed their seats as they sat down.

A waitress arrived at the table. "Water?" she asked.

"Please," Mom said, and the waitress poured glasses all around.

"I'll be back in a moment to take your orders."

"Let's see." Dad scanned the menu. "Tortilla soup, tacos, nachos, quesadillas . . . Chips and salsa to start?"

"Oh, they have peach-mango salsa," Mom said.

"Delicious!" Lulu swung her arms wide, knocking directly into her water glass.

Water cascaded over the table, pooling around glasses and plates. Everyone pushed back in their seats, but Mia didn't move fast enough to keep her shorts dry.

Mom and Dad sopped up water with napkins and the waitress hurried over to help. The table was dry in no time at all, but Mia's shorts weren't quite so fortunate. She sat down, trying not to think about how miserable waiting for soggy shorts to dry would feel. Lulu's bottom lip trembled as she sat down again.

"It's okay, Lulu," Mia said. Lulu nodded, blinking hard.

"Pass me your glass, Mia," Dad said. He filled it up a little less than halfway. "Yours next, Lulu. You too, Maddie. Let's play some music."

He added water so each glass held a different amount. Dad tapped his spoon against the glasses, adding splashes of water until each played a distinct tone. Then he passed them around.

Mia's glass was the high note. Dad motioned for her to start, and taught the girls how to play a simple version of "Three Blind Mice" that used only three notes. They experimented until they managed to hit their spoons just right, so the glass rang out just in time. Soon, they were laughing and having fun again. Lulu had forgotten about the water. Even Mia had almost forgotten about her wet shorts. Also, it helped that the sea breeze had dried her off much faster than she'd expected.

"Can we practice our song for Mom's concert?" Lulu asked.

In London, Mia and Lulu had convinced Mom that they should sing at one of her upcoming concerts. She hadn't chosen which concert they'd present the song at yet, but she had promised that one day they'd sing. Maddie hadn't been thrilled about the idea to begin with, but she seemed to be coming around now.

"Maybe later, when we get home," Dad said. "We'll need more than three notes for that song."

"Everyone smile!" Miss Julia snapped a photo of the girls and their glasses. "And now, who wants to talk about rides at Captain Swashbuckler's Adventure Park?"

"I want to do a log ride. And see penguins. Oh, and cotton candy. I want some cotton candy," Lulu said.

"Do you think they'll have cotton candy at a water park?" Mia asked. "More like saltwater taffy, right?"

"We get cotton candy at the beach sometimes," Lulu said.

"True," Mia had to admit, especially after Maddie caught her eye.

Maddie seemed to have a sixth sense about what would cause a fight between Mia and Lulu. For now, Mia held her tongue. Disaster averted.

"Here's the map." Miss Julia tapped her phone. "On Barrel Buffoonery, you ride in barrels over rapids and down a waterfall . . ."

"Down a waterfall?" Lulu asked. "Cool!"

"I don't know . . ." Maddie said, sounding much more like her usual self. "That sounds dangerous."

"Oh, I'm sure you can count on all the rides being safe," Dad said.

"There's High Jinks on the High Seas," Miss Julia said. "Where you do battle with a pirate ship."

"What? Let me see that." Mia reached for the phone and scrolled through the pictures. "Looks like they teach you to sword fight and everything. The pirates try to take over your ship . . . What's that called?"

"Commandeering," Dad said.

"Also, I have a surprise for you, girls," Mom said. "One of my friends knows a marine biologist who works at the park. Tomorrow, we have an appointment to go behind the scenes and meet some dolphins. We might even be able to feed them."

"Really?" Lulu's eyes went wide.

"What do dolphins eat?" Maddie asked.

"Fish, mostly," Dad said.

Maddie made a face, but Mia grabbed her arm. "Like in *A Ring of Endless Light*! Remember that book, Maddie? How Vicky and Adam went to the research center and worked with the dolphins and . . . Oh! They could speak to the dolphins when they were in the water with them, speaking without even talking! We could swim with the dolphins, couldn't we, Mom? I mean, it wouldn't be that big of a deal, right, if we're already backstage. We can wear our swimsuits—"

Mom cut her off. "I don't think you can swim with the dolphins unless you're trained, sweetheart."

"But it's not like dolphins are dangerous or any-thing. Vicky did it and she wasn't trained . . ."

Mom gave a wouldn't-that-be-nice kind of sideway smile. Mia wasn't about to let it go so easily, but clearly arguing now wouldn't get her anywhere. Maybe tomor-row, then. She could ask the biologist herself.

"So what other rides are there?" Lulu asked.

Mia handed back Miss Julia's phone, but she wasn't thinking about rides anymore. In the book, when Vicky swam with the dolphins, she didn't have to put her thoughts into words. The dolphins simply knew, and talking with them—or actually, thinking with them—was how Vicky made her world right again. It wasn't that Mia's world was wrong, exactly, but it wasn't right, either. Maddie was too far away, as though a door had

closed between them. Mia couldn't exactly ask her
to open it back up. Could she? Not in words. But the
dolphins didn't need words. Maybe if she swam with
them, she'd figure out how to speak without words too.
Tomorrow. She'd find a way to make it happen.

THREE

Stars polka-dotted the velvet-black sky, brighter than usual because the moon was nowhere to be seen.

"Perfect stargazing weather!" Dad said as they walked back toward the bungalow.

Everyone bundled up with sweaters and blankets and went back onto the beach. Even though it was dark, Mia took off her shoes. The sand felt like liquid stone under her feet. She spread out her fingers to let darkness stream through her hands. Maddie and Lulu spread out their blankets next to the beach chairs, and Mia put hers next to theirs.

"There's the Big Dipper," Mia said, pointing it out.

"And there's the Little Dipper," Maddie said.

"What else do you see?" Dad asked.

The Glimmer family had a tradition of inventing star pictures. Dad insisted that the first people who named the constellations were just like anyone else. Who was to say the Glimmer girls couldn't invent new constellations, right here, right now?

"There it is!" Lulu said, pointing. "My starfish flower!"

The starfish flower was Lulu's favorite constellation. She'd invented it on a beach trip three or four years ago. Mia was pretty sure Lulu pointed out a new set of stars each time.

"I see a footprint," Maddie said. "It might be a clue."

"Oooh . . . Like the footprint of someone who stole a star painting." Lulu launched into her Glimmer Girls to the Rescue theme song. "Maddie, when will we solve our next mystery?"

Good thing the night was dark, because Mia knew she'd made a face. It wasn't fair that Maddie had become the detective of the family. Maybe she'd solved the mystery in London, but she'd done it by breaking the rules. Her consequence for rule breaking had been no movie-watching on the flight to San Diego. To Mia, the consequence didn't seem big enough at all, especially since everyone was also treating Maddie like a hero.

"Let's admit, it wasn't a good thing for Maddie to sneak out," Mom said. "But I'm also so proud of Maddie for being brave and speaking up when she knew that something was wrong."

"But she SNUCK OUT!" Mia snapped.

As soon as the words were out of her mouth, she wanted to take them back. She could feel Mom's look even though she couldn't see her face in the dark. Mom had already spoken with Mia about letting Maddie's mistake go. Mia was trying—honestly, she was—but it wasn't easy.

"I see a dancing dolphin!" Maddie moved away from Mia, nudging over to Mom and Dad to draw the imaginary lines of the star picture in the sky.

Mia knew Maddie was intentionally changing the subject. Maddie didn't like it when Mia and Lulu fought, and she was even less willing to argue herself.

"Show me!" Lulu scooted over toward Maddie.

Mia sat up and hugged her knees close, resting her chin on her knees.

"Do you see any pictures, Mia?" Miss Julia brought her blanket over and sat down.

"Not yet."

"You'll never see anything if you don't look up."

Mia could hear the smile in Miss Julia's voice. "True."

"You know what I like best on nights like this— nights without the moon? It's dark enough to see the Milky Way. To me, the Milky Way looks like a stripe of star paint across the sky. It's beautiful because of all the tiny lights shining together. None of the lights are big enough to be spectacular on their own. Or at least not from our vantage point here on the earth."

"Star paint," Mia repeated, following the line of light in the sky. "Wouldn't it be fun to have a can of that?"

"What would you use it for?" Miss Julia asked.

"Oh, everything. My bedroom ceiling and the play-room ceiling, and of course I'd share it with Maddie and Lulu for their bedrooms. And maybe I'd paint a path of starlight from the back door out into the yard. Maybe I'd make a secret hideout. The paint would point the

way so Maddie and Lulu and I could follow the path at night when it was dark enough to see. We could have sleepovers and read stories and drink hot cocoa."

"When I was younger, my dad and I built a clubhouse in the backyard," Miss Julia said. "Maybe when we get home, we could see about making one for you girls in the backyard. We wouldn't have the star paint, but we could have the rest of it—especially the hot cocoa."

It was an idea—a good one. Usually Mia would dive in and start planning, assuming that Maddie and Lulu would love the idea too. But now, she wasn't so sure. "Do you think we'd all like a clubhouse? I mean . . . I'd like a clubhouse. I don't know. Never mind."

"If you'd like one, that's a good place to start," Miss Julia said, and Mia had a feeling she heard the unspoken question about Maddie too. "You know how it feels to watch your mom sing? She's on stage, doing the thing she most loves to do. Joy radiates out of her, and it soaks into the rest of us."

"I can't help but sing along," Mia said.

"Right? And even if music isn't our thing, watching your mom sing makes us think about our own dreams and ideas. We're inspired to think about what brings us joy. We don't have to love the same things to be inspired by one another. When a person creates something, whether it's a song or a clubhouse or a satellite, in her own way, she's celebrating God's creation. She inspires others around her to celebrate in their own way, and on and on it goes, ripple after ripple."

Mia didn't answer for a long moment, playing back Miss Julia's words in her mind. "God wasn't thinking about clubhouses when he created the universe, though."

"Maybe not, but I'm sure he was thinking about each unique one of us. About how I would love strawberries fresh from their vines on hot summer days. Or how you would love curling up with books—"

"And how I would love Doritos!" Lulu announced, plopping down next to Mia.

"Yes," Miss Julia laughed. "About that too."

"Do you think God's ever tasted Doritos?" Lulu asked, her voice loud enough to bring everyone else into the conversation.

"Hmmm," Dad said, chiming in. "Hard to say."

"Well, I hope so," Lulu said. "I hope God can have as many Doritos as he'd like, because they're de-licious."

Miss Julia wrapped her arm around Mia's shoulders and squeezed her tight. "I'm proud of you."

Mia lay her head on Miss Julia's shoulder and thought about clubhouses and star paint and everything between the words too. Maybe she and her sisters were each one of a kind, but she hoped they wouldn't forget how to sparkle and shine together. They were Glimmer girls, after all.

FOUR

The gates to Captain Swashbuckler's Adventure Park looked like giant waves of aqua, blue, green, and gold. As the Glimmer family and Miss Julia stood in the entrance line, two pirates sauntered over. One woman and one man, they both wore striped shirts and gold earrings and swords tucked into their thick leather belts.

"Ahoy, me hearties," said the man. "Who here wants to learn to swing a sword?"

"Me, me, me, oh, me!" Lulu said, bouncing up and down.

Mom eyed the swords. They didn't have sharp edges, but they were definitely made of heavy metal.

"I'm not sure . . ."

"I'm strong enough, Mom," Lulu said.

"We realize you could lift the sword, Lulu. We're just worried about the person you might swing it into." Dad grinned over at Mom, and she shrugged as if to say, *Well, they're asking for it.*

"Let's try that open space over there," the woman said, pointing out a patch of grass. "Your mom and dad can stay in line, and we'll take you three girls together. It will be perfectly safe, I promise."

"Perfectly." The man scrunched an eye and added, "Arrgh."

"Go ahead, girls," Mom said. "We'll hold the space in line."

"I'm on camera duty," Miss Julia said.

"Make sure Lulu doesn't skewer any pirates, please," Dad said.

"Will do," Miss Julia promised.

The sword was heavier than Mia expected. She faced off with the man—he was still scowling. Mia wondered if he knew he was more funny than frightening.

"We pirates, we lift our opposite hand for balance while swinging a sword," he said. "Put yer weight on both feet, that's a lassie, and now raise your sword like this. Swing right . . ."

Mia did, and he countered, their swords ringing as they clashed together.

"Aye, shiver me timbers! Soon ye'll be a fine pirate, sure as that ol' North Star in the sky."

"Look at me! Look at me!" Lulu danced forward with her sword, swinging back and forth wildly. The female pirate countered, backing away. "I'm winning!"

Miss Julia snapped picture after picture. Mia's pirate taught her to parry, to lunge forward and back, and to spin out of the way and duck.

"Want to try, Maddie?" Mia asked.

Maddie shook her head. "I'm learning by watching you."

"How 'bout ye two pirate lassies give it a go?" the pirate asked, holding out his sword to Maddie.

Soon, Maddie and Mia were clashing swords, lunging left and right as though they were in a movie. Lulu stood off to the side and cheered, first for one and then the other. Then Lulu insisted on her own fight, so they each took turns battling it out with her.

"Looks like it's time to go into the park." Miss Julia snapped one last picture.

"Call that one Lulu the Conqueror," Lulu said.

"Make sure ye visit High Jinks on the High Seas," the female pirate called after them. "Yer ready for battle, I'd say, sure as me sea legs."

"Yay!" shouted Lulu. "Shiver me timbers."

Mia and Maddie followed their pirate sister into the park.

"Avast, mateys!" A woman wearing a striped skirt and a shirt with puffy sleeves strode up to them. The beads on the ends of her braids clicked with each step. "Have ye heard about sailing our seven seas?"

Mia exchanged looks with Maddie and Lulu. "Nope."

The pirate held a map open so they could see. "Straight ahead, ye'll find Pete's Paddle Boats—fine gentleman, he. Across the bridge is Buccaneer's Island. No matter what ye need, ye'll find it on our bonny island. Provisions, a hearty meal, treasure . . . even coffee."

"Coffee," Dad said. "Now you're talking."

"Chart yer course across the bridges to each of our seven seas. Ye'll find the Arctic, Indian, Northern Atlantic, Southern Atlantic, Northern Pacific, Southern

Pacific, and Antarctic. Each sea holds adventures of its own, and, of course, ye'll want to keep an eye out for wildlife."

"Like dolphins?" asked Lulu.

"Dolphins, sea otters, penguins, flamingos . . ." She reached into her satchel and pulled out three passports, one for each of the girls. "Pillage or plunder if ye must. But, whatever ye do, make sure the captains of each sea—salty dogs that they are—stamp yer passports. A full passport at sundown yields treasure beyond yer wildest dreams."

"Jewels?" Lulu asked.

"Not real treasure," Mia told her.

"Ye never know, lassie," the pirate said. "Now, where are ye headed?"

"What's that?" Lulu pointed out the ride that towered over all the rest.

"That's Scalawag's Splash in our Indian Sea. But ye must be four feet tall to ride."

"I'm tall enough," Lulu said. "Right, Mom?"

"We haven't measured you recently," said Mom. "It will be close."

"Most of the rides are for riders three feet and taller. I'm sure ye'll be tall enough for those," the pirate said, letting down a little of her swagger to cheer Lulu up.

"Come on, come on, come on!" Lulu said, tugging on Mom's arm. "Let's try Scalawag's Splash first!"

"May the wind be in yer sails!" the pirate called after them.

Lulu urged them on to the right, making a beeline for Scalawag's Splash.

"Where's the captain?" Maddie asked.

"Looks like his station is next to the bridge." Miss Julia pointed out a white-whiskered man who wore a giant captain's hat.

"Welcome, ducks," the captain said. His name tag read, *Captain Whitebeard.*

"Ducks?" Lulu asked. "Is that a pirate word?"

"It's a Captain Whitebeard word," he said, winking. He stamped their passports and passed them back. "Enjoy the Indian Ocean!"

From here they could see a snow-peaked mountain. Boats shot out of a dark opening over a cascade of water and under a bridge. Most of the ride appeared to be inside the mountain.

Lulu's eyes went wide. "Wow."

"Do you think it will be fun?" Maddie asked Mia.

Mia felt a grin spreading across her face. Yes. She was positive it would be fun. "Come on!"

"There's the sign, Lulu," Mom said. "Let's see if you're tall enough."

"I hope she is," Maddie whispered as they walked over. "I don't want to think about—"

A wail cut through her words. Mom's hand was an inch above Lulu's head. Mom shook her head and hugged Lulu tight.

"Then maybe we shouldn't go either . . ." Maddie said.

"You know what I see?" Dad asked. "Lulu, come with me. You girls go ahead. We'll all ride the next one together."

"Stay together," Mom said. "We'll cheer you on from here."

"Do you want me to come with you?" Miss Julia's grimace made it clear that riding Scalawag's Splash was not her definition of fun.

"We'll be fine." Mia reached for Maddie's hand, and as soon as they were out of earshot she said, "They're letting us ride on our own!"

FIVE

Maddie gripped Mia's hand tighter as they went through the gate and into a cave. "Do you think we'll get wet?"

Inside, it was cool and just a little bit dark. Blue and green lights cast a watery glow across the walls. Portholes cut into the stone wall showed off an aquarium teeming with glowing jellyfish. "We'll be okay." Mia laced her arm through her sister's, feeling better than she'd felt all week.

Ahead, voices echoed off the walls. After rounding a few more corners, they found the end of the line just at the bottom of a tall staircase. At the top, a pirate wearing an eyepatch and striped pants with frayed edges greeted them.

"Ahoy, me lassies. How many are ye?"

"Ten?" Mia asked, not sure why he wanted to know their age. Was there an age rule to go along with the height one?

"Ten of ye, hmmm?" the pirate asked, shooting a puzzled look over her shoulder.

"Oh, no, just two," Mia corrected.

"Well then, step right up. This way. Ye'll be in boat number two."

Mia led the way to the boat and climbed into the front seat. Water sloshed around her feet, and ahead a dark cave yawned open.

"You okay?" Mia asked Maddie.

"I guess . . ." Maddie said. "I'm glad you're in front."

The bars clicked down over their laps, and then the boat shuddered.

"Hold tight!" The roller coaster buzz filled Mia's stomach as the boat jerked forward. Darkness swallowed them and the boat tilted back, clicking as they headed up, up, up. "Oh my gosh, oh my gosh, oh my—" *Pfft!* Cold air blasted Mia's face, and cut Maddie off mid-word.

"What was th—" *Pfft!* Another blast of air came from the other side. Still, they clicked upward.

A tiny chittering sound began, growing louder and louder by the moment, along with the whisper of movement—the sound of teeming insects. Of course, there weren't any real insects, but knowing this didn't slow Mia's heartbeat.

"I want off!" Maddie said.

"It's okay," Mia said, but she heard the shake in her own voice. "It's just for fun. I mean, we're having fun, right?"

"Mia, I want off."

She said this at the exact moment the log stopped climbing up. They tilted forward and hurtled forward into the dark. Mia's body went weightless, lifting off the seat, and ripping a scream from her throat. Her stomach stayed far behind. She would have tumbled into the void, were it not for the bar that pressed against her legs, holding her in place. In front of her was darkness, thick as a pool of poster paint, deep as a well with no bottom.

Then, light. Mia whipped her head around to see. Light illuminated a face in the darkness.

Dark shadows gaped under the eyes, sagged in the hollowed cheeks, and filled the wide-open mouth. The horrible face looked just as surprised as the girls felt.

"Mia, Mia, Mia!" Maddie said.

"Hold on!" Mia shouted.

The light clicked off. Then, they were careening around corners, jolting one way and then another. Water sloshed over the sides of the boat with each curve. Mia felt soggy and wrung out, afraid of what might pop out of the darkness next. She was afraid for herself, but especially afraid for Maddie. She could hear real fear in her sister's voice, and she couldn't do anything to help. The clicking began again and they were rising. Light appeared ahead and Mia remembered the waterfall she'd spotted before. They'd come out the opening they'd seen from the outside.

"Hold on, hold on, Maddie!" she shouted.

And they were weightless again, plunging over the side of the mountain, or at least it felt that way. The minute they hit the bottom, a giant wave of freezing water rushed over the front of the boat. Immediately, Mia was drenched from head to toe.

"Maddie! Mia!" a voice shouted from somewhere overhead.

Mia looked up and saw Lulu and Dad standing on the bridge, pointing giant water guns at them. She opened her mouth to tell them to stop, but Lulu blasted her face with water. It was too much.

"Stop it, stop it!" Maddie shrieked.

The boat swirled through the lagoon until they were at the dock. An attendant helped them out of their seats. Most of the other passengers were met by friends or family with towels. Mia huddled next to Maddie and shivered. Soon, Lulu bounded over with Dad, Mom, and Miss Julia close behind.

"Did you see how I nailed you right in the face?" Lulu asked. "Kapow! Perfect shot!"

"Knock it off, Lulu," Mia snapped.

"Mia!" Mom warned, and then saw the looks on Mia and Maddie's faces. "Girls, are you okay? You're soaked."

"We can rent towels on Buccaneer's Island," Miss Julia said. "Be back in a flash."

"What did I do?" Lulu asked, hands on hips. When no one answered, she asked. "Well? What?"

"Nothing, Lulu." Mia said over the chattering of her teeth.

"You know what," Mom said. "I think the ride wasn't quite what the girls expected. But it's just the start of our day and we have so much fun ahead of us. You know, I saw someone with Belgian waffles while we were waiting. Maybe we need a little snack and time to dry off. What do you say, Maddie?"

Despite their sogginess, Dad wrapped one arm around Maddie and the other around Mia. "You'll warm up soon enough, girls. It's going to be a hot day."

"It's not hot now," Mia said.

"True," Mom said.

"Towels!" Miss Julia said, hurrying back with her arms full.

Soon, Mia had a fluffy towel wrapped around her shoulders and they were on their way to Buccaneer's Island for Belgian waffles.

"How are you feeling?" Mom asked Mia.

"A little better," she said.

"You know, I think Lulu would appreciate it if you'd go talk to her."

"She . . ." Mia noticed the droop of her little sister's shoulders. "Right." She hurried to catch up with Lulu. "Sorry for snapping at you, Lulu."

"I wish I could have gone on the ride with you," Lulu said.

"You probably had more fun with the water gun than Maddie and I had on the ride," Mia said. "But we'll make sure the next ride is one we can all go on, okay? Hopefully it will be less scary too."

"The ride was scary?" Lulu asked. "Scary how?"

Mia launched into the full story. Maddie tossed in her two cents every now and again. Even though she'd been more than scared on the ride, now that she was beginning to dry off and warm up, Mia felt brave recounting the adventure. She and Maddie had done it. They'd actually conquered Scalawag's Splash on their own.

SIX

Buccaneer's Island was a circular downtown, surrounded by a moat filled with paddle boats. Bridges, like spokes of a wheel, led off the island into each of the seas.

"Why do those boats keep knocking into one another?" Lulu asked.

"Looks like they're a cross between paddle boats and bumper cars," Dad said. "Look at those foam bumpers!"

"Can we try them out?" Lulu asked.

"Once we've dried out, we'll think about it," Mom said.

Streets led off each bridge, angling straight into the heart of the island. A tall weather vane stood at the exact center. Weather-worn buildings with striped awnings lined the streets. Everything had an old-fashioned flair, as though by entering the park they'd stepped out of the 21st century and into long ago and far away. Here was a seafaring world full of pirates and sailors and women wearing bustled skirts and hats covered with flowers and ribbons. Along the street, Mia spotted a variety of shops. There was an old-time photography studio, a shooting gallery, and a theater that played black-and-white movies.

"The bakery is this way." Miss Julia headed for the center of the island.

Mia followed along, so interested in the various shops that she forgot to shiver. Soon, the smell of warm sugar filled the air. A bell rang on the bakery door as they pushed through and joined the line.

"There's no maple syrup?" Lulu considered the pile of Belgian waffles.

"They're delicious, even without anything on top," Miss Julia said.

"Hmm . . ." was all Lulu had to say about that.

Soon, though, everyone had a warm Belgian waffle in hand, and no one complained. They sat at an umbrella-topped table outside the bakery. The crunchy, sweet waffles were just about as perfect as anything Mia had tasted in a long time. Not so sweet they caused a headache, but definitely sweet enough, and just-out-of-the-oven warm. Now that the girls were dry, Miss Julia snapped a picture of Mia and Maddie, captioning the picture: Our Brave Adventurers.

Miss Julia still had the park map on her phone, but the paper one was much easier for everyone to look at together.

She opened it up and smoothed out the folds. "So, which of the seven seas should we head to next? Each area has rides—one or two—and animals native to the regions."

"I want to see the dolphins and seals," Lulu said, pointing to the part of the park that was closest to the actual ocean.

"Our appointment to meet the marine biologist is at eleven," Mom said. "So we can see the dolphins then. How about sea turtles? Or parrots? Penguins?"

"Yes, yes, and yes!" Lulu bounced in her seat.

"And how about everyone else?" Mom smiled over Lulu's head at Mia and the rest of the group.

"Maybe another ride?" Mia said. "As long as it's a little less wet."

"I want to try out the paddle boats," Lulu said.

"They look fun," Maddie agreed.

Miss Julia collected everyone's towels and locked them in a locker in case they needed them later. Mia hoped they wouldn't need them again, at least not as much as they had after Scalawag's Splash. She'd worn her swimsuit under her clothes so she'd be ready to swim with the dolphins. But even so, it hadn't been fun to have soaked shorts and a tank top over the suit.

The captain of the Northern Pacific Sea had a line, so they went straight to the Pete's Paddle Boat dock. They'd have their passports stamped later. Each paddle boat had two seats. Mia climbed in with Dad, Maddie with Mom, and Lulu with Miss Julia.

"Beat you around!" Mia called to Maddie, and then she looked over at Dad. "Peddle!"

"Why do they call them paddle boats?" huffed Maddie. "Shouldn't we call them peddle boats?"

Mia tossed Maddie a grin over her shoulder. "Betcha can't catch us!"

"Wanna bet?" Maddie called, leaning into it. "Come on, Mom, let's go!"

Sure enough, in just moments, Mia's boat jolted forward. She looked back to see Maddie waving sweetly. "Gotcha!"

"Wait up, wait up!" Lulu called, and then she and Miss Julia rammed Maddie's boat, which rocked Mia's boat all over again.

"Oh, you're in for it now," Mia said, starting to peddle again.

"What are you going to do?" Maddie asked. "You can't bump us . . . You're in front!"

Mia realized this was true. No matter how fast she and Dad went, the only thing they could do was outrun everyone.

"To the right, to the right!" Dad shouted.

They zigzagged across the water, avoiding the other boats. In spite of their efforts, Lulu and Maddie both managed a couple solid hits.

"To the finish line, then!" Mia said.

"Go, go, go!" Dad shouted.

What followed was a neck-in-neck race, but Mia and Dad won by the tiniest bit. Of course, laughter slowed everyone's peddling the whole way.

"High fives all around," Dad said, once they were on dry ground.

"Let's go again!" Lulu said.

SEVEN

We only have a few minutes until eleven." Mom examined the map. "Maybe we can walk through an exhibit on our way—sea turtles, maybe?"

Excitement buzzed through Mia. It was almost time for her to swim with her dolphins. She was sure that all she had to do was to ask. Why would the biologist say no?

They crossed the bridge into the Southern Atlantic Sea area, and another captain waved them over.

"Greetings. I'm Captain Barnacle."

"Isn't that a thing people don't want on their boats?" Lulu asked.

"Well, they gave me the choice between Barnacle and Sea Slug. I decided Barnacle was the better choice." Captain Barnacle winked. "Would you like me to stamp your passports?"

"Please." Miss Julia handed all three over.

"Looks like you're just starting your day," Captain Barnacle noted. "Looking for anything particular in the Southern Atlantic?"

"Sea turtles," Mom said.

"Point your bow toward the port side," Captain Barnacle said, gesturing off to the left. "You can't miss them."

"Cheers!" said Lulu, and everyone laughed.

She'd picked up the expression in London after a long discussion about why Londoners didn't say plain thank you. Mia's laughter cut short—thinking of London made her think about the mystery and about what had happened with Maddie. She studied her sister's profile. It was odd to think that Maddie might be making plans right now, plans she wasn't sharing with Mia. Like Mia hadn't shared her plans to ask for a dolphin swim. *We're each unique*, Mia reminded herself, thinking of her conversation with Miss Julia last night. But couldn't they be unique together?

"What do you think?" Maddie asked, right at Mia's elbow.

"Huh?" Mia looked up and saw the green-blue water behind the glass and the sea turtles gliding past.

"I like their noses," Maddie said. "But do they actually smell things?"

Miss Julia consulted her phone. "Sea turtles have an acute sense of smell in the water. They take water in through their noses and then it flows back out of their mouths—that's all part of their process of smelling."

Lulu opened her mouth to ask something, but just then, Mom said, "It's 10:50. Ready for the dolphins?"

A thrill shot through Mia. "Ready!"

They hurried through the crowds toward the dolphin building. A white-coated woman met them at the door and held out her hand to Mom. "Hi, there. I'm Zarin."

"I'm Gloria," Mom said. "And this is Jack, Miss Julia, Mia, Maddie, and Lulu."

Mia loved the way Zarin's smile spread across her entire face, even lighting up her eyes. "The dolphins are expecting you. And let me tell you, they're excited, because they're ready for their meal. I chose this feeding time for our meeting because I thought that would be the most fun for you."

Mia noted the plaque on the wall. "Why's this called the dolphin and seal hospital?"

Zarin motioned for them to come inside. "Most of the animals in the park are here because they need rehabilitation of some kind. Our goal is to release them back into the wild if we can, once their issues have been resolved. Some of our animals are deemed non-releasable, but we try our hardest to avoid that situation at all costs."

"What kind of rehabilitation?" Maddie asked.

"For dolphins, it's often a torn fin. But one of our dolphins came to us with an infection that made him so weak, he could hardly swim. Surfers found him beached a little south of here, and as soon as we could, we transported him to our facility."

"So the dolphins are all hurt or sick?" Mia couldn't keep the disappointment out of her voice. Zarin wouldn't let her swim with injured or sick dolphins.

"We have two dolphins who are full-time residents," Zarin said. "Those are the ones you're going to meet today, out at the public sea pens. Our dolphins have had a busy morning, swimming with one of the newest dolphins in our care. One of our females arrived with a torn fin, and soon afterward she gave birth to a baby. Since the mother is still healing, our resident dolphins are teaching the baby the ropes. All that playing makes them hungry."

So maybe there was still a chance to swim with them, then.

"Will we see the baby?" Lulu asked.

"From a distance," Zarin said, locking the door and leading them deeper into the building. "We're limiting the baby's exposure to humans so that when she's old enough for release, she has the best possible chance of making it in the wild. When animals are exposed to humans, they lose some of their wildness. They become comfortable near the shore and boats and lose their natural instinct to keep their distance. In the wild, people aren't trained to interact with sea life, and so each of those interactions can be dangerous—for the animals and for the humans."

The wall facing the park was windowless, but windows lined the inner wall. Outside, a network of docks crisscrossed the sea pen area. Beyond the high rock wall was the sea.

"This building creates a shell to protect the hospital area from the public sea pens. We have observation decks so that park visitors can watch the resident dolphins and seals in the public sea pens. The decks are only open for certain hours of the day. We've closed them now so we'll have privacy." Zarin stopped and pointed out a shape in the distance. "There—you can barely see her, but that's our dolphin baby."

Lulu stood on her toes and peered through the glass. "Bobbing her head up and down?" she asked.

"Yep, that's her," Zarin said.

Mia had just spotted the tiny shape before it burst out of the water, arcing up and back down again, revealing its miniature tail fin.

"She's showing off for you," Zarin said. "Almost as though she knows you're here."

Mia realized that what she knew of dolphins may not be scientific. Most of her knowledge came from *A Ring of Endless Light*. But the book had made her think that dolphins could sense other animals, people—and thoughts—from a long way away.

"Do you think she does know we're here?" Mia asked.

"Possibly," Zarin said. "There are still a lot of things we don't know about dolphins. We do know they're highly sensitive animals, to one another and to everything in their surroundings too."

"Why do they jump?" Maddie asked.

"There are a lot of theories. Maybe because air creates less friction than water, so they go faster when they jump. Possibly to get rid of bacteria while they're in the air, or to gain a better view of the sea. Most people who spend any amount of time with dolphins think they jump because they enjoy jumping. They're playing. At least, that's what I see."

EIGHT

Zarin led them past the rest of the windows and through a few locked doors into another hallway.

"The seals are down that way. We'll see them a bit later, but we should start with our hungry dolphins." Zarin led them down one last hallway and out a door onto a wide wooden dock.

The observation decks were high above their heads to the left. Otherwise, the dolphin area seemed just as remote as a private sea cove. Another rock wall divided the dolphin area from the open sea. And then, she saw the dolphins. They seemed to fly through the water as they sped toward the girls. Mia's breath caught. Dolphins, real live ones, so close she could almost reach out and touch them. They tipped back their heads and chittered.

"See, what did I tell you? They're delighted to see you! Ladies, meet Xena and Titania, our resident dolphins."

Zarin grabbed a bucket and loaded it up with fish from a glass tank teeming with them. She swung the bucket onto the deck. The dolphins became even more excited, darting around each other, and splashing their fins in the water.

"If only we could get Lulu this excited about her dinner," Miss Julia said, laughing.

Lulu started waving her hands and dancing around, trying to get first one dolphin and then the other's attention.

"Careful, Lulu," Mom laughed. "You'll end up in the pool with them."

"Could we go in with them?" Mia pounced on the opportunity to ask. "Please, just for a little bit?"

Zarin shook her head. "I'm sorry. Feeding the dolphins is as close as we can get to them today."

"Like she said, they're wild animals," Dad reminded Mia.

"But—"

Mom put a hand on Mia's shoulder. No. Zarin had already said no. Mia shoved her hands in her pockets, wishing now that she hadn't asked like that, out of the blue. She hadn't had the chance to make her case. And now, if she asked again, she'd only get in trouble.

"Here we go." Zarin set the bucket on the dock by their feet.

Fish—living, squirming fish—splashed around in the bucket. Apparently, Zarin expected Mia and her sisters to pluck the fish out of the bucket and throw them to the dolphins.

"Wait, we're going to touch . . . those?" Maddie asked.

"Yep! Who's up first?" Zarin asked.

"Me, me, me!" Lulu plunged her hand into the bucket and tossed a fish to the waiting dolphins.

One raised its head and snapped the fish up in one bite.

Mia could see that the other dolphin was just as hungry. She looked at the squirming fish and back at the dolphins.

"Come on, guys!" Lulu said, grabbing another fish.

Mia figured the best way to do this was to not think about it too much. She shoved her hand into the cold water. The fish were so slippery, all she had time to do was hold tight, yank the fish out of the bucket, and toss it through the air. The other dolphin lifted its head and swallowed the fish whole, and then opened its mouth in a wide smile.

"She's smiling! Maddie, you have to try this," Mia said.

"I don't know . . ." Maddie eyed the bucket of flopping fish with disgust.

"They're slippery, but it's not as bad as it looks," Mia said.

"How about I help you?" Miss Julia took a fish out for Maddie, but almost dropped it as it flipped and flopped in her hands. Maddie tried to grab its tail, but didn't get a good grasp before the poor fish flopped into the dolphin tank. Both dolphins dove for it. That fish never had a chance.

"You did it!" Mia said.

"Kind of," Maddie said, wrinkling her nose.

After that, the girls all started grabbing fish and tossing them, so that soon the air was full of flying fish. Miss

Julia snapped photo after photo. The dolphins ducked and bobbed in a happy frenzy. Mia stopped throwing fish after a while. She wanted to watch the graceful way the dolphins slid through the water. Every now and then, they splashed their fins on the water, begging for more. At one point, they even swam away, flying through the water. They jumped once, twice, side by side in graceful arcs before coming back for more. Mia thought she'd never seen more graceful, amazing animals in her life. She crouched down to look them in the eyes. One swam close, pausing, almost making Mia's heart stop as their eyes connected.

Can you hear me? Mia thought in her direction.

If the dolphin answered, Mia didn't hear what she said.

Once all the fish from the bucket were gone, Zarin asked, "Would you like to see the seals?"

"Sure!" Lulu said.

Mia held back, watching the dolphins swim and play as the others filed inside. Soon, it was just Mom waiting, holding the door. "Time to go, Mia."

It was already over and she'd hardly had a chance to plead her case. "Can I just put in my toes?" Mia asked in a last-ditch effort. "Please?"

"Mia." Mom's voice left no room for arguing.

Mia dragged her feet as she left the deck. She'd been so sure she'd be able to swim with the dolphins. Not just that, but she'd been positive that somehow the dolphins would help her make sense of her questions.

Zarin led the group down the other hallway. Mia needed to be alone, just for a minute.

She felt Mom watching her. She knew everyone was wondering if she was okay. Everyone knew how much she'd wanted to swim with the dolphins. She felt watched and wondered about and just needed some space.

As they passed the restroom, Mia asked, "May I use the restroom?"

"Sure," Zarin said. "When you're done, come knock on that door up ahead. It will be locked, but we'll be right outside."

"Come right out when you're done," Mom said, giving Mia a no-nonsense look.

Mia wouldn't sneak out onto the dolphin deck by herself, but she knew Mom was warning her not to anyway. Mia felt the unfairness of this almost-accusation pile on top of her disappointment. She wasn't the one who sneaked places she wasn't supposed to go.

Mia stomped her way into the bathroom. She took her time, letting the frustration go inch by inch. She'd figure things out with Maddie a different way. And maybe, some other day, she could swim with dolphins. She'd looked one in the eye, and that was something. By the time she dried her hands, she felt a little more calm and ready to face her family.

NINE

When she opened the bathroom door, she heard voices raised in frustration. She held back, closing the door until it almost latched. She didn't want to walk straight into an argument that wasn't any of her business.

"Get over here," a male voice said.

"What's your problem?"

"Look."

"Yeah, the sign-out sheet, I know. So what?"

"You didn't log our time in."

"Well, neither did you."

Mia peeked out to see what the long silence was all about. A boy and girl—teens, actually—stood just outside the dolphin deck door. Mia ducked back behind the bathroom door when the boy seemed about to turn around. Teens were working here with the dolphins? Mia blinked at her fingers, pressed against the halfway-open door. If teens worked here, that meant maybe Mia could too, in a couple years. If she lived in San Diego. But those were just details. She, Mia, could be working with real, live dolphins.

"You know how serious they are about the check-lists right now," the boy said.

"Why are you lecturing me?" the girl snapped. "It's not like I'm the one letting the animals out of their habitats. Do you really think logging our ins and outs will make any difference anyway?"

"You never know," the boy said.

"Sometimes you're the most frustrating person . . ."

"Don't walk away from me," the boy said. "We're not finished."

"I'm finished. Anyway, I have work to do," the girl said.

Their voices faded as the door to the dolphin deck closed behind them. Mia let out the breath she'd been holding. After Mom's warning, she definitely didn't want anyone to catch her skulking around the hallway. She wanted to see the checklist they'd been arguing over too.

Someone was letting the animals out of their habitats? Her heart began to beat faster, and faster still. A mystery of her own, and an opportunity to help the dolphins. What could be more perfect than that? The checklist hung on a peg just outside the door. On the checklist, boxes labeled in and out had initials and times written on them.

"Mia?" Miss Julia's voice called.

"Coming," she called, hurrying toward the seal door. Caught red-handed. She'd definitely taken too long.

"Did you get lost?" Miss Julia asked. "We were getting worried."

"Sorry," Mia said, not wanting to explain about the argument and the mystery, at least not yet. First of all,

she didn't want to get in trouble. Also, somehow she'd
stumbled into a real-live mystery of her own. Did she
have to share it? She tucked this question away. She'd
think it over and decide. Soon enough, she'd know the
right thing to do.

Three seals lounged on rocks in the public seal area.
They barked at one another and then splashed into the
water to cool off before climbing back up onto the rocks.
Mia had to admit, their whiskered faces were cute,
but they were nothing like the dolphins. Once they'd
watched the seals for about fifteen minutes, Zarin led
them back down the hallways, past the sea pens, and
out into the park.

"Where are you off to now?" Zarin asked.

"What do you suggest?" Dad asked. "The girls wer-
en't fans of Scalawag's Splash, but we had a lot of fun
on Pete's Paddle Boats."

"Scalawag's Splash is definitely the darkest, scariest
ride in the park," Zarin said. "You started with that?"

"Probably not the best choice," Mom said. "The girls
didn't enjoy getting soaked, either."

"It's starting to get hot, though," Dad pointed out.

"If you don't want to get wet, but you want to cool
down, maybe try Iceberg Float," Zarin said. "That's over
in the Antarctic Ocean area, so it's all the way on the
other side of the park, but worth the walk. The ride is nice
and cool, and there's also a not-to-be-missed surprise."

"Let's go, let's go!" Lulu said, clapping her hands.

Mom laughed and reached for Zarin's hand. "Thank you so much for introducing us to the dolphins, and the seals too. You made the girls' day."

"Yes, thank you!" Mia and her sisters chimed in.

"It was my pleasure," Zarin said.

As they crossed Buccaneer's Island, Dad pointed out that it was lunchtime. There were many small restaurants, so everyone got to choose what they wanted. After browsing, the girls decided it was too hot for anything but smoothies. Mia chose orange-raspberry, Maddie chose pineapple-strawberry, and Lulu chose blueberry. They also shared a giant pretzel with melted cheese. Mom, Miss Julia, and Dad had fish tacos. Once everyone had eaten, they headed over the bridge into the Antarctic Ocean area.

Captain Australis stamped their passports and pointed them on their way. "Smooth sailing to you!"

Iceberg Float was at the far corner of the park, and most of the crowd hadn't found their way there yet. The tunnels leading into the ride were white and cool, making Mia think of the inside of an igloo. Soon, they reached the loading area. Each iceberg held up to six people, so everyone piled in and buckled their seatbelts. Then, they floated into the cool darkness. The air filled with the sounds of sea winds and waves. Blue and green light swallowed the darkness as they floated into a large cavern. What followed was a series of caves, each of which looked to be made of ice.

Along the way, staged scenes featured animals, scientific outposts, and other sights one might find near the South Pole. Mia hadn't thought much about what might be at the South Pole, but as they floated she caught her breath over and over. There was an otherworldliness to the dazzling coldness, to the ice and the creatures and the landscape. Ahead, she heard oohs and aahs, but before she could wonder too much about them, they floated into a new cavern, this one dome-shaped.

"Look up!" Lulu shouted, unnecessarily, since everyone was already looking.

Across the ceiling, blue, green, purple, red, and yellow lights danced.

"What is that supposed to be?" Maddie asked.

"The southern lights," Miss Julia answered.

"Like the northern lights?" Mia asked.

"Yes, they show up at the South Pole too," Miss Julia said. "The phenomena is almost identical to what happens at the North Pole. It's caused by solar winds colliding with gases in the upper atmosphere."

"It's beautiful," Maddie whispered.

Sure, it was just a light show, probably not anything like the real southern lights, but after having floated through the dazzling coldness, Mia felt the line between real and imaginary blurring. It was almost as though her family had floated out of the park and into the wild southern sea, to witness a miracle staged just for them. She reached for Maddie's hand and held tight. For a second, it felt like the door between the sisters swung wide open again. No one spoke as the lights continued to undulate in the sky. Their iceberg floated across the wide expanse of the room and back into the darkness.

TEN

Coming back into the noise and brightness of the park was jarring. Mia blinked as her eyes adjusted. The heaviness of the mystery she hadn't shared weighed down on her. She should tell her sisters, but now they'd be mad that she'd waited so long to spill the secret. No one seemed in a hurry to do anything next, so they wandered down the sidewalk into the middle of the Antarctic square.

"Look!" Lulu said, pointing to a gathering crowd. Mia rose onto her toes, trying to see over heads.

"Are they supposed to be doing that?" Maddie asked.

"Is who supposed to be doing what?" Mia asked.

Then, as a tall man leaned over to speak to his son, Mia saw it too. Rather, she saw them.

Penguins, black and white, with orange and yellow markings on their heads, beaks, and necks too. They paraded across the bridge toward Buccaneer's Island, as though they planned to pick up crab sandwiches for lunch. One by one, the penguins hopped up from the bridge itself onto the railing. On they waddled, waving their wings and bobbing their heads.

The crowd laughed and snapped pictures, but Mia was pretty sure Maddie was right to question if they were really supposed to be loose. Surely, the penguins weren't supposed to be out of their habitat all alone, crossing the bridge onto Buccaneer's Island. What if someone touched them and got oil on their feathers that wasn't supposed to be there? What if someone fed them something they weren't supposed to eat? Worse still, what if somehow the penguins got loose and then got lost? Zarin had said all the animals were here because they couldn't live on their own in the wild. Mia assumed this meant the penguins too. Anyway, what would happen to a penguin left on its own on a blazing hot San Diego beach?

"I'm sure they're not supposed to . . ." Mia's voice trailed off as a park truck pulled up.

Four staff members, all dressed in the same white-jacketed uniform that Zarin wore, jumped out with buckets of fish in hand. Three of them were women, and one was a gray-haired man. They moved quickly, the youngest of the women and the man clearing a path through the crowd. The others tossed a fish or two to the penguins. The fish immediately captured the penguins' attention. They about-faced, hopped off the railing, and waddled along behind the biologists. To see them now, you'd guess they went on parade every day.

"Where are you off to?" a man in the crowd called.

"Penguins will be back in the Chill Zone shortly," said one of the biologists. "You're welcome to follow us there."

As the two young biologists passed by, Mia saw the other heft her bucket and mutter, "Third time this week."

The first biologist shot her colleague a look and then forced a bright smile at the crowd. "See you soon!"

"Maybe they planned to do that?" Maddie asked, after the penguins had all passed by.

The man and the woman who'd been crowd-wrangling climbed into their truck and headed for the penguin exhibit.

"Seems unlikely," Miss Julia said. "Penguins on parade all by themselves? The biologists didn't act like it was a planned thing, anyway."

Before she thought about what she was saying, Mia blurted, "Someone's letting animals out of their habitats, and no one knows who."

"What?" Maddie asked.

"No one knows who? A mystery!" Lulu launched into the Glimmer Girls theme song.

Dad caught her arm before she danced straight into a passing family. "Whoa there, kiddo. I'm not sure the Glimmer family needs to be solving any more mysteries."

"We certainly don't need any Glimmer girls sneaking off anywhere." Miss Julia eyed each of the sisters in turn, her eyes stopping when they landed on Mia.

"I didn't sneak off!" As soon as Mia said this, she realized she had snuck off, a little. She'd gone to look at the check-in list without telling anyone. But that wasn't anything like sneaking halfway across London.

Miss Julia raised an eyebrow, but didn't say anything.

"What do you say we find another ride?" Mom suggested. "I'd like to try out Whitewater Canyon."

"I want to see the penguins," Lulu said. "I hardly got to see them out here. Plus, there might be clues near their exhibit—you know, about whoever let them out."

"We don't know—" Dad began.

"Come on!" Lulu grabbed Mia's arm and pulled her in the direction the penguins had gone.

"Why do you think someone would be letting the animals out of their habitats?" Maddie asked Mia, hurrying to catch up.

"Maybe it's just to be funny," Lulu said, giving a twirl. "Ooh, or maybe someone is trying to steal the animals to sell them for lots and lots of money. Or they're keeping them as pets . . . Maybe someone wants to swim with the dolphins even more than you do, Mia."

Maddie's face crinkled with worry. "Not dolphins. That would be so much worse than letting the penguins parade around the park. I think the only place to let the dolphins out would be into the open sea. Though I'm sure they couldn't jump over that rock wall. It was too high, right?"

"I don't think the dolphins are in danger," Mia said. "But when I was coming out of the bathroom, I heard two teens talking about new rules for logging into and out of the exhibits, because someone has been letting the animals out of their habitats. Though they were going into the dolphin area, so I guess it's possible that all of the animals are in danger."

She stopped walking right in the middle of the sidewalk, and Miss Julia bumped into her. "Oof!" Miss Julia scrambled to pick up her floppy hat and pull it back over her wild curls. "Goodness, Mia. Is anything the matter?"

"No. Maybe. I don't think so," Mia said.

"Did you see a clue?" Lulu looked every which way as though she was trying to see the clue too.

"No clues," Mia said. "Not yet."

"Then what are you waiting for? Let's go!" Lulu said, grabbing Mia again, this time not letting go.

Mia allowed herself to be pulled along, but her mind wasn't anywhere near her feet. She'd let everyone in on the secret. Fortunately, no one had been mad she'd held out for so long. But now, the mystery wasn't her own— her special secret—anymore. Still, she could be the one to solve it, even if her sisters knew about it. If she could just figure out why someone was letting the animals out, it wouldn't be that hard to then figure out who was making all the trouble. It would be a very good start, at least. And that was all she needed—just a start.

ELEVEN

A white arch curved over the entrance to the Chill Zone, which was designed to look like the outside of a snow-covered cave. As they walked through, air-conditioning blasted down on their heads. It felt like walking through an air-conditioning waterfall. On the other side, they found themselves in a snowy landscape. As in, real snow crunched under their feet and drifted down from high above them in the darkness. Or, if it wasn't real snow—because how could it be—it was as close as inside snow could be. Cold, and the tiniest bit wet. When one landed on Mia's tank top, its crystal pattern sparkled in the light.

"Well, I don't know about clues," Dad said. "But you sure picked the right place to be on a hot day, Lulu."

"How do they make it snow?" Lulu held out her hand to catch a flake. "Look! They melt just like real snowflakes."

"How do they keep the room from filling up with snow?" Maddie asked.

"Looks like it falls pretty slowly," Miss Julia said. "And down there, near the glass, the snowflakes are swirling around. Maybe there's some kind of air flow. Perhaps a gentle vacuum to pull some of the snow out of the room."

"I think they should let it fill up enough so we could make a snowman," Lulu said.

"My ladies, your penguins." Dad bowed and presented the glass like a queen's herald announcing the arrival of an important guest at the ball.

Sure enough, the penguins were filing back into their habitat. The observation area was a little lower than the exhibit floor, so viewers could see directly into the penguin's swimming pool. Snow-covered rocks circled the water.

"I don't know why they'd want to leave their nice, cool exhibit to walk around in the blazing hot sun," Maddie said.

"Look at that one!" Lulu pointed to a penguin that had clambered out of the water. She was now hurrying around the line of penguins, cutting in front, and diving in again.

"Do you think the line means anything?" Maddie asked. "I mean, is she cutting everyone?"

"How do you know that's a girl?" Dad asked.

"No one knows, with penguins." Miss Julia didn't even have to look this fact up. "The only way to know is if you actually see one lay an egg."

"I say it's a girl," Maddie said. "Won't the others be mad?"

"They don't look mad," Lulu said.

The same penguin shot across the pool, popped back out again, and once again waddled her way to the front of the line.

"Maybe she's a little sister, so they're used to it," Mia said, and then shrugged off Maddie's warning look.

"Mmph!" Lulu said. "Maybe she's an older sister, and they're used to her bossing them around."

"I never boss—" started Mia.

"Whoa there, girls," Dad said.

"Don't forget: Glimmer girls, sparkle and shine," Mom said.

"But most of all, be kind," finished Maddie.

Most of the time, Mia loved their family motto, but not so much when Maddie used it against her.

"Look!" Lulu said. "There's a man in the habitat. Do you think he's the one letting the penguins out? Look at him. He definitely looks shifty."

"Shifty?" Mia asked, eyeing him. "What does shifty look like, exactly?"

"You know, like shifty eyes," Lulu explained, demonstrating.

"How can you even see his eyes?" Mia asked.

Maddie's head whipped back and forth between her sisters as she watched this whole exchange. Mia knew Maddie was uncomfortable and was looking for a way to make the peace.

Miss Julia put a hand on Mia's shoulder. "So, these are Emperor Penguins, the tallest of all the penguins. They live in Antarctica—not surprising, given that we're in the Antarctic Ocean area." She scrolled down on her phone, and then her eyes lit up. "Wow. They can stay submerged under the water for eighteen minutes while hunting."

"Hunting for what?" Maddie wanted to know.

"Most of the time, for fish," Miss Julia said. "And krill and squid."

"He's leaving the exhibit," Lulu said, her voice flat with disappointment. "And he's leaving the penguins behind. I guess he's not the criminal."

"He wouldn't kidnap a penguin in front of everyone," Mia said.

"I guess not," Lulu said. "But how are we supposed to even start solving the mystery? We have no clues. At least at the museum in London, we saw Mr. Hughes take the painting."

"He didn't actually take it," Maddie pointed out. "I mean, not the way we thought."

"Yeah, but looking for Mr. Hughes led us to the real thief in the end. Whoa, look at this!" Lulu fished a soggy piece of paper out from under the snow. "Now this might just be a clue. A real one, Mia."

"Lulu, this is serious." Mia almost rolled her eyes, but caught herself just in time.

Eye rolling was a major offense in the Glimmer family. Most of the time, the eye-rolling rule was no problem for Mia. There was something humiliating about someone rolling her eyes at you. Mia would rather a person speak her mind, instead of acting as though there weren't words to describe how dumb something was that you'd said or done. And it wasn't that Lulu was being dumb, just that she was making the mystery seem like it wasn't a real mystery at all. It wasn't a game. They'd all seen the penguins on the loose with their own eyes. Maybe penguins were easy enough to round up, but some of the other animals would be more of a problem. Like parrots, who could actually fly away. Or seals, who might waddle right into the ocean and never come back.

"Isn't anyone going to look at my clue?" Lulu insisted.

Mia sighed and held out her hand. "Let's see it, then."

The scrap of paper was more interesting than Mia had expected. Rather than being a random receipt, the paper looked like it had been torn from a small spiral notebook. Only part of the words at the top of the page were visible, the rest having smeared in the melting snow. "Pe" and then near the end of the line, "sche," with the rest blurred. Underneath, someone had made a list, only one line of which was still visible: 11:45 am.

"Sche . . ." Maddie read over Mia's shoulder. "Schedule?"

"I think so," Mia said.

"Told you it was a clue!" Lulu leapt into the air and skidded in the snow as she landed.

"All right," Dad said, catching her. "That's enough sleuthing for now. What do you say we try another ride? I've had my eyes on that log ride."

"I want to ride with Daddy!" Lulu said.

"It's a deal," he said.

Mia slipped the paper into her pocket. Honestly, she didn't think it was a clue, but there was the slightest, itsy-bitsiest chance that it was. She didn't have any better place to start. And what Lulu had said was true. Last time they'd solved a mystery, their first theory had been completely wrong. But by following all the wrong clues, they'd found the right ones. Maybe that would happen again. She might as well keep her eyes open for other scraps of paper to match, just in case.

TWELVE

Rather than crossing back through Buccaneer's Island, they took the side path into the Southern Pacific Sea area. Before heading to the log ride, they took their passports to the captain.

"Does anyone have a coin?" the captain asked. Her name tag read, *Captain Coin*.

Miss Julia had a few. She handed them over, and Captain Coin showed the girls how to use her machine to stamp a starfish into the coin's surface.

"Is this why they call you Captain Coin?" Lulu asked.

"It's one reason," Captain Coin said, her eyes twinkling. "Also, here in the Southern Pacific Seas, we have a wishing well. If you toss in a coin and make a wish, they say the winds will grant you your heart's desire."

"We're headed off to the log ride," Dad said. "The girls are wondering if they'll get wet."

"Not soaked," Captain Coin said, "but definitely splashed."

"Maybe we should let the girls warm up a little more first, then," Mom said, and then explained to Captain Coin. "We just visited the Chill Zone."

"Gotcha," Captain Coin said. "Well, if you need something to do in the meantime, you can see live starfish and many other fascinating creatures in our tide pools. They're just past the well, over in that direction."

"Tide pools it is," Dad said. "And then the log ride."

As they passed by the wishing well, Mia asked, "Is it bad to make wishes? I mean, obviously the wind doesn't grant them . . ."

She considered today's list of wishes. First of all—of course—swimming with the dolphins. Since that hadn't worked out, the top of her current list was to find clues and eventually solve the mystery of why the animals were being let out of their habitats. Could she wish, *I wish to know what sche . . . means, and whether it matters?*

"I think wishes are okay, as long as you know them for what they are," Mom said. "What do you think, Jack?"

Dad hoisted Lulu up onto his back for a piggyback ride. "I've made my share of wishes. Like wishing for Mom to fall in love with me, back when we first started dating."

Mom laughed. "Here's what I think, Mia. Wishes are much like prayers. Only, sometimes people get confused about who they're wishing to. For instance, they wish to the winds—rather than to the one who can actually give miraculous gifts. When you pray about your dreams, you're putting your heart's desires into words. Even though God already knows our desires, he still wants us to whisper them into his ear. Think about how it feels to tell a friend—or a sister—something you truly, truly want. Sharing makes you closer, doesn't it? And sharing our hearts with God works that same way."

Dad chimed in, "There's a verse that says, 'Take delight in the Lord, and he will give you the desires of your heart.' "

"Always?" Lulu asked.

"No, not always," Dad answered. "That's the other thing about wishes. God isn't a genie who must grant our wishes. Sometimes we wish for things that wouldn't be good for us in the long run. And other times, granting a wish might take away someone's free will, which God doesn't do either. He couldn't force Mom to fall in love with me, for instance. She had to decide that on her own."

He set Lulu down and scooped Mom into his arms, giving her a kiss.

"Maybe I'll make a wish, then," Mia said, but when everyone turned to look at her, she added, "Later." She definitely didn't want to make a wish with an audience watching.

Like the sea pens, the tide pools made the most of the park's location, right on the ocean. Now that they'd seen most of the park, Mia realized that it had been built on land that jutted out into the ocean. Water, in various small coves and inlets, surrounded about two-thirds of the park. Here, natural tide pools lay scattered among craggy rocks. High tide had swept a variety of sea creatures into the pools of salt water. A marine biologist roamed the rocks, identifying the various creatures for visitors. Maddie's favorites were an orange starfish and several purple sea anemones. Lulu wanted to watch the crab that scrambled around one pool.

"Poor crab," Miss Julia said. "He can't wait to find his way back to the sea."

In another pool, they found a live sand dollar. In some ways, though, it was hard to get excited about tide pools with tiny, ordinary creatures. Just an hour or so ago, they'd been feeding real, live dolphins.

Mia kept her eyes open for clues, but didn't see anything. No random notes, no biologists talking in whispers, or even people with shifty eyes. The thief had no reason to bother with the tide pools, anyway. These animals weren't officially property of the park.

"Ready for the Log Plunge?" Dad asked, after they came to the last pool, this one empty.

"Let's go!" Lulu shouted, and raced ahead.

"Wait for us!" Miss Julia called after her.

There was a short line, but soon they loaded up into three logs. Dad and Lulu in one, Maddie and Mom in the second, and Miss Julia and Mia in the third.

"You ready for this?" Miss Julia asked as they started up a steep incline.

Mia's stomach flipped over, but this time in a good way. It felt different being in a log with Miss Julia than it had being in the boat on her own with Maddie. That morning, Mia had felt responsible for both of them.

Now, she could just relax into the experience. Nothing bad would happen—nothing more than a little splashing, that was. Up and down and around wild corners, Mia laughed all the way through, even when they hit the water at the end and water splashed up over both sides of the log. She and Miss Julia got a little wet, but, as Captain Coin had promised, not soaked.

"Again!" Lulu said the minute they'd climbed off.

The line wasn't too long, so they rode again, switching up so that Mia rode with Mom, Maddie with Dad, and Lulu with Miss Julia. Afterward, they examined the map.

"We haven't been to the Northern Pacific Sea area," Maddie said. "And they have sea otters there."

"What does a sea otter look like?" Lulu asked.

"Like a seal, but furry," Miss Julia said.

Now, here was a chance for clues. "Yes, let's go see the sea otters!" Mia said.

"We don't have to go across the island to get there," Mom said. "We can meander the path and then go see the captain for your passports. Sound good?"

"Good!" all three girls agreed.

Mia rolled her coin in her hand, and as they passed by the well, she tossed it in. *Please, God, help me solve this mystery.* She had no idea if God answered prayers like this one, but she had to at least try. *It's for me, kind of, because I want to solve a mystery of my own, like Maddie. But it's also for the animals. I don't want them to be in danger.*

THIRTEEN

Maddie held back in order to walk with Mia. "Was your wish about the mystery—whether you can figure out who is letting the animals loose?"

"Kind of."

If the non-answer bothered her, Maddie didn't show it. "Did you see anything in the tide pools?"

"No. I'm not surprised we didn't, though. No one is going to take starfish or sea urchins out of there, right? I mean, it's not like they're valuable enough to steal and sell, and what would they do with them? Put them in buckets and dump them in the sea?"

"Why do you think someone would be letting the animals out in the first place?" Maddie asked. "You think it's for money?"

"I don't know. If someone were trying to steal animals, you'd think they'd take them right away. Why would they go to all that trouble and then just let them wander around the park?"

"Ugh," Maddie shuddered. "What a horrible idea . . . Someone stealing the animals and selling them. But, do you think maybe it's someone playing a practical joke?"

"It's a lot of effort for a joke," Mia said. "And it sounds like the problem has been going on for a while now, so that makes it seem more serious to me."

"Sleuthing, girls?" Miss Julia asked, dropping back to join their conversation.

"Just thinking." Mia scanned the faces of kids, moms, dads, grandparents, random park workers—all headed one place or another.

Was one of them an animal thief? A group of teens passed by, jostling one another and laughing. Practical jokesters?

"How many people do you think come to the park every day?" Maddie asked.

"I'd guess thousands," Miss Julia said.

Maddie frowned. "But whoever is letting the animals out must be coming day after day."

"Or they work here," Mia said.

"Stamps, ladies?" the captain at the entrance to the Northern Pacific Sea area asked. His tag read, *Captain Swashbuckler.*

"You're Captain Swashbuckler?" Mia asked.

He took off his hat and bowed low. "At your service. Have you been enjoying my park?"

"Absolutely," Maddie said. "We're going to see the sea otters right now."

"Ah, some of my favorites," said Captain Swashbuckler. "Shake a leg, then, and enjoy!"

The way to the sea otter exhibit was through a darkened building, its walls housing giant aquariums with various kinds of fish. They even walked through a glass arch filled with water, and spotted jellies that glowed in the dim light. The jellies contracted and then stretched long and thin, floating through the water. Mia stopped to watch, mesmerized.

"Come on, come on!" Lulu said. "The sea otters are up here."

They arrived at the viewing area just as a biologist stood up to give a talk. There were four otters in the large enclosure, a giant pool ringed with rocks.

"Sea otters are endangered animals," the biologist explained. "And these have been deemed non-releasable, so they will live here for the rest of their lives. While they're here, they do important work, such as help teach the public about their species. They also mentor young pups that may one day be reintroduced to the wild."

"What does that mean—non-releasable?" Lulu wanted to know, stumbling a bit as she repeated back the marine biologist's word. She did raise her hand, but didn't wait to shout out her question. The biologist smiled, not seeming to mind.

"Good question. All our otters were rescued as young pups. Some pups can be mentored by our older otters and then released. But even though these had mentors, in the end, they didn't learn the necessary skills to survive in the wild. We tried to release Lola, for instance—she's the biggest of our otters, weighing about fifty pounds. Unfortunately, she kept climbing onto surfers' boards out in the ocean. She was too comfortable with humans, and living in the wild was dangerous for her, and for people too. So, now she's here with us."

The otters kept in constant motion. They scratched their backs on the rocks, rolled around, and flopped onto their bellies to slide into the water. In and out they went, often floating on their backs when they were in the water.

"They have so many whiskers!" Lulu said, pointing to an otter that had bobbed back up to the surface with a sea urchin in its paws.

The exhibit had a set of double doors, but no one lingered near them. Maybe the thief wasn't cruel enough to set animals like these free, since scientists had deemed them unable to survive on their own. At least, Mia hoped that was true.

"They act like puppies," Maddie said, laughing as she continued to watch. "Are they related to dogs?"

"Actually, they're in the same family as skunks and weasels," Miss Julia said.

"But not as stinky!" Lulu said.

"You don't know that," Mia pointed out. "They're pretty far away, and behind glass."

"They're too cute to be stinky," Lulu said.

"Skunks are pretty cute too," Miss Julia said. "But you're right, sea otters don't use stink as a defense the way skunks do."

Maddie touched Mia's arm and nodded toward a man with a white jacket, winding his way through the gathered crowd. He made a few notes in a file and then went through the exhibit door into the backstage area.

"What do you think?" Maddie asked.

"I don't know . . ." Mia said.

"Let's remember what he looked like, anyway," Maddie said. "Tall, salt-and-pepper hair, beady eyes."

"Beady?" Mia couldn't help smiling at this.

"Who has beady eyes?" Lulu asked.

"No one, never mind," Mia said.

"Hmph," Lulu said. "No one ever tells me anything."

"So, the Whitewater Canyon ride is here in the Northern Pacific," Mom said. "Or we can try out High Jinks on the High Seas in the Northern Atlantic."

"Anyone ready to show off their sword-fighting skills?" Dad asked.

"Let's go to High Jinks!" Lulu pulled out her imaginary sword and demonstrated some of her moves. "En garde!"

"Whoa, there!" Dad caught Lulu before she slammed her arm into a passing stroller.

"I'm glad she's on our side." Miss Julia laughed. "Okay, Glimmers, this way!"

FOURTEEN

Lulu pretended to sword fight half the way to High Jinks, and then ran out of steam. "You're dragging your heels, Lulu," Miss Julia said. "Hungry?"

"Starved," she said. "For cotton candy!"

Thank goodness Mia wasn't the only hungry one. They stopped for cotton candy for Lulu, and soft-serve ice cream for Mia and Maddie. Mom, Dad, and Miss Julia had a few bites of everyone's treats.

They tossed their napkins and headed off for High Jinks again.

"Excuse me," a woman said, causing everyone to turn. "I'm sorry, but are you Gloria Glimmer? My daughter and I saw your daughters and then you and your husband, and we thought, could that be . . .? We're coming to the concert later this week, so we knew you were in town."

Mom gave them a warm smile. "Yes! You're right. This is my husband, Jack, and our girls, Mia, Maddie, and Lulu."

"Fantastic!" The woman prodded her daughter forward, who looked just about Maddie and Mia's age. "This is my daughter, Stella, and I'm Meredith."

Stella looked at Mom and then at the girls. "Will you sign my . . ." She looked up at her mom, and all at once seemed to realize she had nothing for Mom to sign.

"Actually, I have our concert tickets in my purse," Meredith said. "They'll let us keep them if you've signed them, won't they?"

"Here, I'll sign the part that doesn't tear off," Mom said, signing with a flourish.

"Thank you so much," Meredith said.

"Yes, thank you," Stella echoed, and then to the girls, she said, "It must be fun to have a mom who's a singer."

Mia thought of the travel, the special opportunities like seeing the dolphins, the way it felt to watch Mom sing. How could she explain all that? In the end, she just nodded and agreed. "It is fun."

For once, Lulu didn't have anything to add. Maddie smiled her agreement.

"Our favorite song is 'When I Leave the Room,'" Meredith said. "We hope you'll sing that one tomorrow night."

"That's our favorite too," Mom said.

"Did you know that the show ends with fireworks tomorrow night?" Dad asked.

"Fireworks?" Lulu said, not so speechless now. "We get to stay for the end of the concert, then, don't we?"

"We'll talk about it," Dad said, but he smiled the way that he always did when he definitely planned to say yes.

"We're off to see the sea otters," Meredith said.

"We were just there," Lulu said. "Did you know that sea otters are like skunks?"

"In some ways," Miss Julia hastened to add.

"Fascinating," Meredith said. "Thanks again, and what should we say about the concert . . . Break a leg?"

"Exactly," Mom said. "Thank you."

Meredith and Stella headed toward the Northern Pacific, and the Glimmers went to have their passports stamped in the Arctic Sea.

"Captain Polaris, at your service, ladies. Shall I stamp your passports?" the captain asked.

"Please!" the three girls chimed.

The pirate stamped their passports and waved them onward toward High Jinks on the High Seas. "Smooth sailing to you!"

They lined up for High Jinks. Mia scanned the ground for scraps of paper, but saw nothing but a candy wrapper. She threw it away, trying not to get discouraged. A clue would show up; she was sure it would.

High Jinks on the High Sea was a three-part ride. In the first part, they watched a short movie about the longtime pirate rivalry. The movie told a story of two ships that had been at battle for as long as anyone could remember. Next, the pirates took the group to a training room, where they split the visitors into groups. Along with most of the other visitors, Mia, Maddie, and Lulu practiced stage sword-fighting moves. Mom and Dad learned to operate giant water cannons. A select few, including Miss Julia, learned key phrases, such as "incoming, starboard," or "batten down the hatches!" The pirates assigned these visitors to be lookouts.

The visitors and a few pirates loaded onto the boat that waited on shore. Mia gripped her sword with white knuckles. Worry and excitement tangled inside her, making her arms break out in goose bumps. Would she know what to do when they got out to sea?

As soon as the other boat sailed into the lagoon, she started to laugh. Everyone did. The other pirates were a disaster. They fell over one another, some even falling overboard. Then, they dragged themselves out of the water and back up the ropes. Watching them was like watching a comedy routine.

From her perch on the high ledge, Miss Julia shouted, "Incoming, starboard!"

At this, her hat flew off her head and sailed down to the ship's deck. Mia started for the hat, but just then, a few of the pirates from the other ship swung across the gap between the boats. She raised her sword and fell into the staged battle. The pirates did more falling and somersaulting than anything else. They looked so clumsy, but they always seemed to be in control, which made Mia think they must be acrobats. After Mia, Maddie, Lulu, and the others had captured the ten pirates who had boarded their boat, they loaded them onto a rowboat.

Everyone helped lower the boat to the water, and then they counted down. On one, Mom and Dad doused

the rowboat with their water cannons. Everyone cheered.
After giving one another a high five, Mom and Dad
turned their cannons on the pirates across the way.

"Retreat!" the pirates shouted, each voice rising
above the next. "Retreat!"

The defeated ship pulled away, and everyone cheered
again as they sailed to shore. Even though Mia knew the
battle had been pretend, she couldn't help feeling proud.
Mom and Dad had soaked the pirates, and she, Maddie,
and Lulu had held their own in the sword fight.

"Ready for a rest?" Mom asked. "It's almost time for
the water show. It starts in about half an hour. And then,
time to go home for dinner and bed."

"Just one more ride?" Lulu asked. "I really, really
want try Alligator Ambush. You get to blast the alligators with water guns!"

"Who says?" Mom asked.

"The pirates," Mia explained. "When Lulu couldn't
choose between the water cannons and the sword fight-
ing, they told her she could blast water at alligators on
that ride."

"Sounds fun to me," Mom said.

"But not real alligators, right?" Maddie asked.

"They're too serious about conservation and safety
around here to use real alligators for a ride, sweetheart,"
Dad said.

"Race you!" Lulu said, and she would have taken off
if Miss Julia hadn't caught her arm.

"Remember, no running off, right?"

Lulu sighed as they took off at a more reasonable pace. "Right."

Mia realized she'd become so focused on the battle, she hadn't looked for clues since the ride began. Now the day was almost done, and she hadn't solved the mystery—her mystery. She decided not to miss a thing on the way to Alligator Ambush.

FIFTEEN

Y ou okay?" Maddie asked Mia.

"Yeah." Mia took the paper out of her pocket and studied the blurred writing. "Still no real clues."

"There was that man at the sea otters," Maddie said. "But I'm not sure he was doing anything wrong."

"I guess they wouldn't want park visitors to see any problems. I just thought maybe we'd see something they wouldn't. I've been looking for scraps of paper they might think were garbage. Or something like that, I guess. We don't have much to go on."

"Maybe Dad's right, we should let this one go," Maddie said.

Easy for her to say. She'd already solved her mystery. Mia tried not to make a face. What she needed to do was pay attention on their walk over to Alligator Ambush. Snapping at Maddie wouldn't make finding clues any easier.

"Welcome to the Northern Atlantic Sea!" a man wearing a gold-tasseled coat called, pulling Mia out of her thoughts. His name badge read, *Captain Doubloon*.

"We passed this way earlier, but were in such a hurry we didn't get our passports stamped," Miss Julia said.

"Well, we'd better fix that!" Captain Doubloon said. "Hand them on over."

Soon, they had the final stamp on their passports. The day was so close to being over. *A clue, any clue. Please,* Maddie prayed. *Just one clue.*

"And where are you off to, my friends?" Captain Doubloon asked.

"Alligator Ambush," Dad said. "We're told that's where sailors do battle with alligators."

"Right you are," Captain Doubloon said. "And a valiant cause that is too. To starboard, my friends, to your right."

He saluted them, and they all saluted back. He followed this up with a bow, which they all repeated, as though they were playing an odd, silent game of Simon Says. When he put his thumb to his nose and waggled his fingers, they all burst out laughing rather than following his lead one more time.

"Godspeed to you," he said, and waved good-bye.

"What does that mean, Godspeed?" Maddie asked.

"It's an old blessing that means, 'God go with you,'" Miss Julia said.

"He does anyway, doesn't he?" Maddie asked. "Without anyone telling him to?"

"Yes. I think the reminder is more for us than it is for him," Dad said.

As they walked, Mia found three pennies, one quarter stamped with a starfish, and an abandoned park passport. But no clues.

Drooping vines hung over the entrance to Alligator Ambush. Sounds of birds and wind rushing through tall grasses greeted them as they walked inside. The boats were big enough to hold six, with three rows, and three water guns on either side of the boat. One water gun for each rider. The boat had a screen at the front to record how many times they hit alligators with the water.

"Top score is fifty-three hits," the guide said. "Good luck."

"Ready, girls?" Dad said as they floated through the swampy entrance and onto the river.

Mia peered down the barrel of her water gun, wanting to be first to spray an alligator. To her right, a yawning set of teeth rose out of the water.

"Fire!" she shouted, squeezing the handle.

"Three hits. Four!" Dad called, as everyone on the right side of the boat fired away. The alligator slipped back under the river's surface, as though they'd frightened him.

"On your left!" Mom shouted, and everyone on the other side of the boat aimed at the new alligator who'd dared to lift his head.

A knocking on the bottom of the boat almost stopped Mia's heart, until she remembered. "They're not real alligators!" she called to no one in particular.

Left and right and then right again, the alligators kept on coming. "Forty!" Dad called. "We can do this!"

But the end of the ride was approaching. Mia could see the landing area looming ahead. Two last alligators popped up, one on either side of the boat. Everyone shot away, giving those monstrous jaws all they had. When they arrived at the landing area, they'd made fifty-one hits.

"Nice work!" the guide said, helping them up and out of the boat. "Want to give it another go?"

"We're headed for the five o'clock water show," Mom said. "Or else we would."

Miss Julia took their picture underneath their score. Even though they hadn't won, she captioned the picture: Victory!

"That was fun, fun, fun!" Lulu said.

Mia pulled her little sister into a giant hug. It had been fun, fun, fun. And now, they were off to the water show. Chances were, she wasn't going to find any clues at the show. Which meant it probably was time to let the mystery go, no matter how much she hated that idea.

"What's the hug for?" Lulu asked.

"Because," Mia answered. "Glimmer girls, sparkle and shine, but most of all . . ."

"Be kind!" her sisters chimed.

Mia linked her arm through Maddie's and then through Lulu's. Enough trying to solve the unsolvable mystery for now. Dad was right. The park prankster, or criminal, or whoever he—or she—was wasn't Mia's responsibility. She'd tried to pay attention, but she'd come up with a big, fat zero. Nothing. Inside, her prac-tical self battled this out with her hopeful self. *Please, just one clue,* she thought. *Anything. And also, I need to let it go.*

"Are you okay?" Maddie asked.

"It's been a good day," Mia said, not exactly answer-ing the question.

"Even if we only shot the alligators fifty-one times." Dad sighed.

Mom shook her head and gave him a sideways squeeze. "Let it go, Jack."

"We did give those pirates the what-for." Dad wrapped his arm around her and squeezed her back.

"Water show is this direction," Miss Julia said.

"Lead the way," Dad said.

SIXTEEN

Mia and her family found seats near the High Jinks lagoon for the show. While the Glimmer family rode Alligator Ambush, the park staff had transformed the lagoon. A long, narrow dock now floated in the middle of the water, housing a scaffolding with lights and speakers. Overhead, two scaffolding arms bridged the distance from the dock to sturdy beams on the shore. A stage jutted forward from the dock, set to look like a rocky shore with various platforms at different heights.

"Ladies and gentlemen, the show is about to begin," an announcer's voice boomed over the loudspeaker. "Please find your seats."

People shuffled to find seats. Soon, the music began with cymbals and brass, rising to a crescendo, and then two balls of flame burst out of the sea. A bass drum rolled, and spotlights focused on an actor who stood on the highest of the rocks.

"I'm here to tell ye the tale of Captain Swashbuckler the Bold," he boomed, his voice magnified over the music. "I must warn ye, it's a dreaded tale full of fire and fury, but if ye stick with us to the end, ye won't be disappointed."

At this, the music swelled again. One of the two pirate ships sailed under the scaffolding to the center of the lagoon.

"Avast, Cap'n," a sailor shouted from the crow's nest. "The Jolly Roger, she approaches."

"We're under chase!" another shouted.

"It started like any other day at sea," the storyteller said. "But as the ship flying the pirate flag approached, she seemed to be running on a phantom wind."

"We're becalmed, Captain!" one of the sailors shouted.

"What's becalmed?" Lulu asked Miss Julia.

"That's when there's no wind," Miss Julia answered.

"But the other ship has wind?" Lulu wanted to know. "Why?"

"Watch," Dad said.

The other ship swept into the lagoon, and battle ensued. Mia saw every sword move she'd learned, and many more. Pirates swung onto Captain Swashbuckler's ship in wave after wave until the sailors shouted, "Abandon ship. Abandon ship!"

"Captain Swashbuckler wasn't one to give up his ship without a fight. He stood his ground, alone on his ship's deck," the storyteller continued. "Finally, the pirates overpowered him."

"Walk the plank!" the pirates shouted.

"'Twas a sight to see, watching this battle-hardened captain walk his own plank."

"I know not what magic you've used to becalm my ship and overcome my men," Captain Swashbuckler shouted, his hands bound, and his feet standing at the end of the plank. "But hear this! You haven't seen the last of me!"

He stepped off the plank, and the pirates jeered. The two ships sailed away.

"Everyone assumed Captain Swashbuckler had gone down to Davy Jones's locker," the storyteller said. "But they were dead wrong."

"What's Davy Jones's locker?" Lulu asked.

"The bottom of the sea," Dad whispered. "He means that everyone thought Captain Swashbuckler had drowned."

Before Lulu could ask anything else, four fins appeared in the water, moving fast.

"Are those dolphins?" Mia asked.

Two winged creatures swung out over the sea. It took a moment for Mia to realize they were actors, not giant seabirds. Nearly invisible ropes hooked them into the scaffolding beams.

"They're flying!"

"They're jumping!" Maddie pointed out.

The fins weren't attached to actual dolphins, either. Swimmers in costume worked together to leap out of the water in arcs, mimicking dolphin leaps almost exactly. After watching for a while, Mia saw that they were pushing off one another to catapult themselves into the air. Meanwhile, the birds spun and circled overhead. Their ropes were stretchy, allowing them to dive into the water and spring back up, dripping but safe. On one of the dives, a bird came up with Captain Swashbuckler in her arms. He was limp and bedraggled. The bird delivered him to the dolphins, who propped his head up and helped him swim to the rocky shore.

"Early in his days, Captain Swashbuckler had saved a dolphin," the storyteller said. "And in return, they had promised to keep him safe. So, they carried him to shore. The seabirds watched over him by day and the dolphins watched over him by night. Soon, he gained his strength back."

"By what magic did those pirates take my ship?" Captain Swashbuckler shouted, raising his fist. "By what power did they seize the winds?"

"For weeks, no answer came," the storyteller said. "But one day, the seabirds whispered in the captain's ear." At this, the birds swooped down on either side of the captain. The storyteller continued. "They told the captain tales of his ship, now flying the Jolly Roger and full of cruel-hearted men who terrorized the sea. Birds and fish alike had seen Captain Swashbuckler's courage as he fought these men. Now, the creatures had devised a plan to help him take back his ship."

Again, the ship flying the Jolly Roger sailed toward the lagoon. This time, the pirates shouted with fear. "Avast! Where sail we? Turn, turn!"

The water around the boat teemed with swimmers in silver and gray and black. Dressed as dolphins and whales and seals, they propelled the ship into the waters in front of Captain Swashbuckler's island.

"The pirates' ill-gained magic betrayed them," the storyteller said.

At this, water rose on all sides of the ship, creating a curtain of water. The seabirds lifted Captain Swashbuckler off his rocky shore, and he rose high into the sky above the ship.

"Between the unnatural water and the unlikely sight of Captain Swashbuckler hovering over their ship, the pirates panicked. They climbed over one another in their haste to abandon ship."

As the last pirate dove overboard, the seabirds set Captain Swashbuckler onto the ship's deck. The curtain of water fell back into the sea, and the dolphins and other creatures began to swim and leap. Seabirds danced in the sky. Again, the music swelled as Captain Swashbuckler raised his sails.

"From that day forward, a pod of dolphins led the way every time Captain Swashbuckler set sail. Not one pirate dared touch his ship again," the storyteller boomed.

The ship sailed out of the lagoon to a final refrain of music.

"Wow," Lulu said, as the final applause died down and they stood up to go.

"Want to add some water and fire to your next show?" Dad asked Mom.

"No, thank you." She laughed. "Though that was spectacular, I must say."

Mia thought that if she couldn't be a dolphin trainer, then maybe she'd want to be an actor playing a dolphin. "Do you think it's hard to swim like that?"

"Terribly," Dad said. "But anything is possible with practice."

"I'd want to be one of the birds," Lulu said. "Or a pirate. En garde!" She raised her imaginary sword, and Dad scooped her up onto his shoulders before she impaled anyone in the crowd.

"A well-spent day," Dad said. "But now it's time to cash in those passports. Onward, Glimmer girls!"

On their way out of the park, they showed their completed passports to the pirate at the gate. She gave them the choice of dolphin pendant necklaces or pirate hats. Lulu chose the hat, but both Mia and Maddie chose necklaces.

"It's the perfect treasure," Maddie said. Mia had to agree.

SEVENTEEN

Mia woke up in the dark. For a moment, she didn't know where she was. Then she heard waves breaking outside her window and the pieces fell into place. The beach bungalow. San Diego. Her dream had been of a lone dolphin, injured, trying to outswim a shark. She'd found herself eye-to-eye with the dolphin—a real one, not one played by an actor. It was as though she could hear the dolphin's thoughts, feel his terror. She shivered, goose bumps crawling from her shoulders down to the tips of her fingers. Even if it was only a dream, she couldn't shake the feeling that she needed to do something, anything, to help the dolphins and the park's other animals. Before it was too late.

"What's wrong, Mia?" Maddie whispered, rolling over to face her sister.

Like in London, the twins were sharing a king bed. Even though it was plenty big for all three girls, Lulu had chosen the trundle bed. This was fine with Mia, because Lulu always flailed in her sleep.

Mia pulled the covers tight around her shoulders. "Nothing."

"Nightmare?" Maddie asked.

"It's not right, the animals being let out."

"When I asked you to run across London with me, chasing after Mr. Hughes, you did. I'll help you, Mia, if you want me to."

If she wanted her to. Mia heard the question in Maddie's voice, and realized she wasn't the only one who felt the distance between them. Now was the time to say something. Only Mia couldn't think what to say.

Finally, she said, "What if we convince Mom and Dad to let us go to the park again tomorrow? Lulu's scrap of paper might be a clue after all. Maybe it's a schedule of when someone planned to let the animals out. Or something."

"Maybe. We can try," Maddie whispered. "It's their date day tomorrow—they said we could choose together what to do as long as all three of us agreed."

"So all we have to do is convince Lulu?" Mia's mouth quirked up in a smile. Just convince Lulu; no big deal.

"We didn't ride all the rides," Maddie said. "She may say yes."

"Okay." Mia lay back down. "And Maddie? Thanks."

It was the best she could do, as close as she could come to saying that she loved her sister and wanted things back the way they used to be. Why was the truth so hard to say? Maybe because it wasn't a fair thing to want, Mia realized. No one stayed the same forever.

"Mmm . . ." Maddie murmured, already halfway back to sleep.

Mia wasn't nearly as quick to fall asleep. She rolled ideas around and around in her mind, trying to come up with the perfect way to convince Lulu that going to the park would be the perfect way to spend their day, trying not to think about everything that felt so different between her and Maddie.

When she opened her eyes the next morning, Mia blinked. Why was she so tired? Then, it all came rushing back—her dream, her talk with Maddie, and their plan to convince Lulu to go back to the park. Maddie's side of the bed was empty. When she peeked over the side of the bed, Mia saw that Lulu's trundle bed was empty too. She pulled on a pair of shorts and a tank top, and went in search of her sisters. She found them out on the sand, making a multilevel sand castle.

"Maddie said you wanted to go back to the park today," Lulu said.

Mia couldn't tell from Lulu's expression whether she thought this was a good idea or not. "We didn't ride the Undersea Treasure Dive or the Bermuda Triangle ride yet," Lulu said.

"Plus, we didn't go see the walrus," Maddie added, clearly trying to be helpful. "Or the parrots."

"And I want to ride the alligator ride again," Lulu said. "Even without Dad, it would still be fun."

Miss Julia opened the screen door and crossed the sand to join the girls. "What are you girls chatting about?"

"Mom and Dad said we could choose what to do today, right?" Mia asked. "Because they're having a date day?"

"Yes," Miss Julia said. "I was wondering if you girls would like a day to play on the beach."

"Well," Mia said. "What if we went back to the Adventure Park?"

"I don't know . . ." Miss Julia said, glancing back at the bungalow. Mom and Dad were in the kitchen, cooking breakfast.

"We didn't ride all the rides," Lulu said.

"Is that why you want to go back?" Miss Julia nailed Mia with a probing look. "Not because of an unsolved mystery?"

Mia traced a line in the sand. "Well, if we happened to find some clues, I wouldn't be upset."

"Wait. We're going to look for clues all day?" Lulu asked. "No way. We already did that yesterday."

"We did not spend all day looking for clues," Mia said. "We hardly found any clues at all."

"Except the one I found, the one you said wasn't a clue," Lulu shot back, almost knocking over the sand castle as she added her next handful of sand.

"Well, now I'm not so sure," Mia said. Lulu gave her a disbelieving look.

"Honestly, Lulu." Maddie shored up their sand castle from the other side. "Mia told me last night that she thought your schedule might be important."

"If it's the thief's schedule, it's definitely important," Mia said.

"So, if we go back to the park, are we only looking for clues?" Lulu pressed.

"We'll ride rides," Mia said.

"And see animals too," Maddie said.

"If," Miss Julia pointed out, "your parents say it's okay. But you girls all want to go?"

"Yes," Mia and Maddie said immediately.

They both looked at Lulu with please-please-please in their eyes. "Fine," Lulu said. "Yes, I want to go."

Maddie and Mia grabbed Lulu's hands and twirled her around. Miss Julia went inside to check with Mom and Dad. Soon, all three were back.

"I'm not sure I like this newfound passion for solving mysteries," Mom said. "Last time—"

"Last time we solved the mystery!" Maddie said.

"Right, by sneaking out," Dad said. "I know it's intriguing to hear about a problem and it's natural to want to solve it, but this mystery is none of our business, girls."

"But can't we just go back to the park to have fun?" Mia asked. "And if we see a clue, then we see a clue?"

"As long as you girls promise to follow Miss Julia's instructions. Keeping track of three Glimmer girls in a park all by herself won't be the easiest thing to do. I expect you to make her life easy by sticking close and listening. *And,* if you don't see any clues today, you need to let this mystery go. Deal?"

Mia threw her arms around Mom and Dad in a giant hug. "Deal. Thank you, thank you, thank you!"

EIGHTEEN

When they arrived at the park, the pirates were already busy training someone else to sword fight. Mia didn't mind. Today, she didn't need any distractions.

"Do you think there's only this one entrance into the park?" Mia asked. "Could the criminal be coming in through here?"

The woman in front of them turned around and eyed the girls.

"Maybe he needs a code name—you know, so we don't attract too much attention calling him a . . . *criminal.*" Maddie whispered this last word.

"Or her," Mia said, remembering the London thief.

"Or her," Maddie agreed.

"What about Dr. Dolittle?" Lulu asked.

"But Dr. Dolittle helped animals," Mia protested.

"It's actually a pretty good code name," Maddie said. "*Doctor* could be male or female, and maybe this person is trying to help the animals, in his or her own way. You never know."

"But letting the animals out—" Mia said, cutting herself off when the same woman turned and looked again.

"Shhh . . ." Lulu said, drawing even more attention.

"I know!" Mia whispered. "Okay, fine. Dr. Dolittle isn't helping the animals, that's all I'm saying."

"Do you think Dr. Dolittle comes in through the front gate?" Maddie asked. "Wouldn't they start to notice the same person coming in every single day?"

"Especially if he had shifty eyes," Lulu said, demonstrating, just as she had the day before.

Then she broke into her mystery-solving theme song. So much for being on the down-low. At that moment, the ticket attendant called them over, gave each a ticket, and stamped their hands.

"Didn't I see you here yesterday?" the woman asked, confirming Maddie's suspicion about the park attendants noticing people. "Your necklaces gave you away."

Mia fingered the dolphin pendant around her neck.

"We loved it so much, we had to come back," Miss Julia said.

"Where will you start?" the woman asked. "Favorite rides or animals?"

"Cotton candy!" Lulu announced, making everyone laugh.

"Actually, I think we're off to the Underwater Treasure Dive," Miss Julia said. "We didn't have time for that one yesterday."

"That's one of my favorites. While you're down there, be on the lookout for the golden key. Oh, and speaking of . . . There's a day two challenge instead of passports." The woman handed over three rolled-up scrolls. "Have fun!"

As soon as they'd moved out of the way of the incoming crowd, Lulu unrolled her scroll. "Ooh! A treasure hunt."

Mia and Maddie checked out their scrolls. Sure enough, the challenge was to find fourteen items scattered across the park. Once found, they should fill in the blanks with the locations. If you found at least eight by the end of the day, you could choose a prize.

"We might not have time to find all these," Mia warned. "Not if we're looking for clues too."

"But we'll be looking so closely at everything that we'll probably find clues *and* all the treasure," Lulu insisted.

Mia had a feeling the treasure hunt was going to be a disaster. Lulu would be on a mission, dragging them all over the park, rather than letting her follow any real clues that showed up.

"Come on, Mia," Maddie said. "It will be fun. And Lulu's right, the treasure hunt will give us a reason to keep paying close attention."

"Ooh, and look!" Lulu pointed toward the center of Buccaneer's Island.

They'd all seen and heard the weathervane at the center of the park, with its spinning gears and chimes and colorful trinkets. Now, looking again, Mia saw what Lulu had spotted.

Maddie had seen it too. "There's a dancing penguin on top!"

One item spotted, thirteen to go. They all wrote it into their scrolls and passed them back to Miss Julia.

"Should we start with the Underwater Treasure Dive, then?" Miss Julia asked.

Mia followed her sisters and Miss Julia, dragging her heels. She was positive they wouldn't find any clues in the Underwater Sea Dive. But, afterward, maybe they could go check out one of the animal exhibits. As she walked, she ran through the park map in her mind. She had almost memorized it on the way to the park this morning. Parrots, penguins, flamingos, seals, sea turtles, maybe sea otters. She would focus on the animals that could actually go somewhere if they got out of their exhibits.

Underwater Treasure Dive was in the Southern Atlantic Sea area. Since they'd already done the passport thing yesterday, there was no need to stand in line to talk to Captain Barnacle. The line for the ride was short. Soon they sat, along with about ten other people, in a miniature submarine.

"Do they really mean underwater?" Maddie asked. "As in, we're going underwater now?"

As the motor whirred to life, they plunged down, down, down. Yep. Really and truly underwater. After the first wave of bubbles cleared away from the portholes, the water was clear—a sparkling aqua. It teemed with a surprising number of fish.

A Dolphin Wish

"There's a zebra fish," Maddie said. "And a clown fish."

"But where's the golden key?" Lulu asked.

"Is that an octopus?" Maddie asked.

"It might be," Miss Julia said. "A small one. I think I see eight legs. Actually, an octopus has two arms and six legs, but they all look like legs to me."

"I can't see the golden key." Lulu leaned forward and backward in her seat.

"Keep your eyes open," Miss Julia said. "I'm sure we'll see it. In the meantime, let's enjoy all these fish. Look at that bright red one. What's that, I wonder?" She tapped her phone. "No Wi-Fi down here. I'll have to look it up later."

Fish of all shapes and sizes swam past the window, some of which they could name. Miss Julia kept telling them to remember this or that fish so they could look it up later. Once they had circled the cove, the submarine began to rise.

"It's over?" Lulu asked. "But we didn't see the golden key!"

"It's only one of the fourteen items," Miss Julia said. "As long as we find eight, you can still earn your prizes. Plus, think of all the fish we saw."

Lulu folded her arms, not in the mood to be cheered up. "Hmph."

Maddie put her arm around Lulu and pulled her close. "It's okay, Lulu."

The submarine's motor shut off, and the captain came out of his little cockpit to open the hatch and let them all out. Everyone stood to go, but something in his hand caught Mia's eye. When no one but Mia was watching, he hung it on the wall just outside the cockpit door. A large golden key.

NINETEEN

Mia thought about writing the location of the golden key into her scroll. She also thought about telling her sisters what she'd seen. But one look at Lulu's pout, and Maddie anxiously trying to cheer her up, made Mia decide not to. Maybe later, when they were almost done with the hunt, she'd tell everyone what she'd seen. But not now. For now, the golden key was her secret.

"Can we go see the seals now?" Mia asked.

"Sure," Miss Julia said. "What do you say, Lulu? We didn't see the ones outside the hospital yesterday. They're over in the cove right next to where we saw the dolphins."

Mia checked the map and led the way. Miss Julia looked up the fish they'd seen. "That grumpy looking gray-green fish with the orange spots and the puffy lips was a monkey-faced eel." She showed the girls as they walked. "And guess what the one that looked like a lemon was?"

"An ocean lemon?" Maddie asked.

"Close!" Miss Julia laughed. "A sea lemon."

"Is it actually a fish?" Maddie asked.

Miss Julia studied the screen. "No, it's an invertebrate. Like an octopus or a snail, and, apparently, it has a citrus smell and acidic taste, just like an actual lemon."

Mia looked up from the map. "A living, thinking lemon? Weird."

"I'm not sure about the thinking part," Miss Julia said. "But living, yes. Ooh! Remember that rainbow fish with the bulging eyes and the delicate fins? That was a coralline sculpin."

Maddie leaned over to look. "That one was my favorite, I think. How about you, Lulu—did you have a favorite?"

"Mmph." Lulu still wasn't over the key.

Mia felt a twinge of guilt. But honestly, the treasure hunt was a game, wasn't it? And weren't games about winning? She would obviously tell her sisters if either of them needed one last item for their lists. But it would feel good to have found something no one else had. Particularly if she ended up not solving the mystery. As this thought floated through her mind, Mia remembered the dolphin from her dream and his dark, frightened eyes. No. Not solving the mystery wasn't an option.

"Whoa!" Maddie stopped to take it all in.

Ahead, a wooden platform overlooked a rocky cove peppered with seals. Open ocean stretched beyond the inlet. A natural arch of stone broke the waves before they foamed their way into and out of the cove. The seals barked to one another, some splashing into the water to swim and others climbing back up onto the rocks to lounge in the sun.

"How does the park keep the seals from swimming away?" Lulu asked.

"Looks like they have made their own decision and chosen this for their home," Miss Julia said.

Mia scanned the crowd. Seeing nothing more interesting than a few families snapping pictures, she checked the platform's wooden beams. No crumpled papers or clues of any kind. Then, she spotted a man in a white jacket walking toward the nearby dolphin buildings. He pulled a key card out of his pocket.

"Excuse me?" she called, hurrying after him.

"Mia, wait!" Miss Julia said. "What are you doing?" Behind her, she heard the others right on her heels.

"Excuse me, sir?" she called again. This time, the man turned.

"Can I help you?" he asked, smiling in a reassuring way at Miss Julia.

"Does the park feed the seals?" Mia asked.

"You mean the ones in the cove?" The man shook his head. "No. It's actually illegal to feed wild seals. Even if it weren't, we wouldn't feed them. We want them to remember how to hunt for their own food, to stay wild, the way seals should be."

"So why don't they just swim away?" Lulu asked.

"The cove protects them from predators, such as sharks. Actually, the seals chose this cove before we built the park here. We worked hard to shield their habitat during construction, and, thankfully, they stuck around. Our seal cove is a benefit for our visitors, a chance to see animals in the wild. Our biologists appreciate it as a natural lab to study the wild seals. Also, after we rehabilitate injured or sick seals, the cove provides a safe space for release. Here, our seals can reengage with wild seals. It's an ideal situation."

"Thank you," Miss Julia said to the man, and then to the girls, "We should let our friend go back to work. And I see that the Barrel Buffoonery ride is just around the corner. What do you think—shall we go ride?"

"That's one of my favorites," the man said. "Have a fantastic day at the park!"

He swiped his card and headed into the building. Mia followed her sisters past the barking seals and toward to the ride. While they'd spoken with the biologist, a boy with a backpack had joined the crowd. He leaned over the rail, watching the seals. He might not have caught her attention, except for the fact that he looked just about her age—maybe a year or two older—and he wasn't with any adults. Strange. Her parents definitely wouldn't let her or Maddie wander around a park on their own. But maybe he was older than he looked.

The barrel ride opened up to another little cove, so that the barrels landed in salt water. Attendants in rowboats guided the barrels back in to the deck, where riders could climb out. The rest of the ride meandered like a river, sometimes lazy, other times frothing with wild water. As they got closer, Mia saw each rider got their own barrel.

"Let's check your height," Miss Julia said to Lulu.

Mia was grateful when Lulu's head measured at least two inches above the line. It would have been another disaster had she not been tall enough to ride.

Right after stepping away from the measuring stick, Lulu pointed to a sign painted with a cartoon octopus who appeared to be singing. "A singing octopus—that's on the treasure hunt!"

Sure enough, it was. The girls jotted down the sign on their scrolls, and then handed them back to Miss Julia for safekeeping. As they stood in line, Mia thought about the seals. She'd have to cross them off her list of endangered animals. The seals in the cove didn't belong to the park, so they wouldn't be in danger from Dr. Dolittle. The seals in the hospital might be in danger, but no one would be cruel enough to mess with a sick or injured seal. Would they? Mia supposed it depended on what kind of criminal Dr. Dolittle turned out to be.

Soon, it was their turn to climb into barrels. As soon as her barrel spun away from the dock, Mia couldn't think of anything but holding on. Even though Mia could tell the barrels were designed not to tip over, it felt like every other second she was about to tumble over the side and into the water. She laughed and shrieked along with her sisters as they bobbed

down the river, and then burst over the short falls into the cove.

"Mia, look!" Lulu shouted, motioning to the ocean-facing side of Mia's barrel. A slick gray head bobbed just out of reach—a seal!

Mia leaned over the side of her barrel to look the seal in the eyes. "Hey there, you."

He—or possibly she—stayed put, blinking once, twice. Then he dove back under the water and swam out into the sea. What kinds of stories might a seal tell? How far might he have traveled in his life? Just around this bay? Across the ocean, maybe even to Hawaii? Had he narrowly escaped a shark at some point? Made friends with a puffer fish? As the attendants guided Mia's barrel toward the shore, she watched the horizon, hoping for one more glimpse of her seal.

TWENTY

T hat was awesome!" Lulu bounced in circles around Mia as soon as she climbed out of her barrel.

"It was awesome," Mia agreed.

"Let's look for treasure and have some cotton candy!" Lulu said.

"It's still a little early for cotton candy," Miss Julia said. "Maybe a Belgian waffle?"

No one complained about this suggestion. As they crossed the Northern Atlantic bridge onto Buccaneer's Island, Lulu stopped and stared at her shoes.

"What?" Mia asked.

"Look!" She pointed to a plaque set into the wooden boards beneath their feet. "A queen starfish!"

Sure enough, it was a starfish with a crown, and another treasure for the hunt. They found an empty table where they could add the treasure to their scrolls. Miss Julia went to buy waffles, and they held the space.

Maddie waited until Miss Julia was out of earshot and then said, "Here's what I think we should do. We know our way around the backstage area where they keep the dolphins. And that's where Mia first heard about the mystery. If we sneak back there, we might be able to find those teenagers Mia heard talking yesterday. We could ask them questions. Or we can just poke around and look for clues."

"Ooh!" Lulu bounced in her seat. "Super sneaky spies!"

Mia shook her head. "No way. We promised Mom and Dad we would listen to Miss Julia."

"You can't solve mysteries by following every single rule," Maddie said.

"You never used to be like this, Maddie," Mia said, her accusation popping out before she could think it through.

"Like what?" It was Maddie's turn to be surprised. Lulu watched one sister and then the other, eyes wide.

Mia wanted to backtrack, but she'd already begun— she decided she might as well try to explain. Still, the words didn't come easily.

"Like . . . I don't know. Someone who breaks the rules whenever you feel like it."

"But don't you want to solve the mystery?" Maddie asked. "I thought the whole reason we came today was to find clues and solve the mystery. Anyway, I don't break the rules whenever I feel like it. When have I broken the rules today?"

"I don't know. I'm not saying you— Never mind." Mia's leg shook with pent-up frustration. "I do want to solve the mystery, but I want to do it the right way."

"And how are we supposed to do that?" Maddie demanded.

"I don't know. I . . . Wait."

"What?" Lulu asked, and then she shook Mia's arm and repeated, "What?!"

"I have an idea! The schedule," Mia said. "It was a feeding schedule, probably, right? And it was a clue, Lulu, a very important one."

Lulu cocked her head. "What do you mean?"

"Zarin said the animals eat at specific times—on a schedule—right?"

"Right," Maddie said.

"So, if someone walked around the park, watching what time the animals were fed, they'd know when someone is with the animals and when the animals are alone. The feeding times would be the times you wouldn't want to mess with the animals."

"Or let them out!" Maddie broke into a smile. "That means, if we figure out when the animals are being fed—"

"And when they're not," Mia put in.

"Then we know when to watch the animals, when they're most at risk of being let out of their cages!" As soon as she'd said this, Maddie's face fell. "But wouldn't there be a lot of feeding times? Multiplied by all the animals? How would we keep track and be in the right place at the right time?"

"It won't be easy," Mia said. "But at least it's a start. It's the first real idea we've had, right? Now, I'm sure we can find more clues. Don't you think?"

"Maybe . . ." Maddie sounded a long way from sure.

"Glimmer girls to the rescue!" Lulu said.

At least Lulu was into the idea. If nothing else, maybe she'd go along with looking for clues for a little while rather than only wanting to try all the rides. Mia didn't mind riding—she liked the rides, even—but she couldn't let another day go by without finding answers.

"Dr. Dolittle, here we come!" Lulu said, pumping her fist in the air, and making both of her sisters laugh.

"What did I miss?" Miss Julia asked, returning to the table with a tray of Belgian waffles.

For a few moments, all conversation stopped as the girls reached for the waffles and savored the warm sweetness.

"Thank you, Miss Julia," Maddie remembered to say, after her final bite.

Mia swallowed her last bite and nodded. "Yes, thank you."

"Mmmmm," was all Lulu could add, busily chewing away.

Mia took Lulu's scrap of paper out of her pocket. "What time is it?"

Miss Julia checked her phone. "11:45."

"Penguin feeding time is 11:45, or at least that's what I'm guessing the time on Lulu's scrap of paper meant. So, maybe we should go over there now."

"But you said we should go when they weren't feeding." Maddie frowned. "I don't get it."

"If it was me . . ." Mia bit her lip, thinking it through. "I'd wait until the feeding was over. I'd watch as the biologists left, and wait until no one was in the exhibit, anywhere. And then, when it was safe, that's when I'd let the animals out."

"Because any other time, someone might be walking through?" Maddie asked, more a statement than a question.

"Right," Mia agreed. "It's the safest time for Dr. Dolittle, and the most dangerous time for the animals."

"Off to the penguins, then!" Lulu said.

"Yes, off to the penguins!" Mia said.

"Hold on a second," Miss Julia said. "Let's clean up our mess first."

"Okay, but we need to hurry." The more she thought about it, the more Mia was sure her theory was right on. Now was the time when Dr. Dolittle was likely to strike.

She helped her sisters wipe the extra powdered sugar off the table and onto their trays with napkins. Then, they stacked the trays in the dish bin.

"Now?" Mia could hardly stand still.

"Okay, now. But keep together!" Miss Julia called. "And walk!"

They slowed their jogging to what could almost be called a walk, but which probably still would have counted as an Olympic sport.

"Goodness, girls," Miss Julia said, hustling to keep up. "Good thing my legs are longer than yours or I'd never keep up."

"Hurry, hurry, hurry!" Lulu urged.

Soon, the Chill Zone was in sight.

TWENTY-ONE

There must be a back or side door. Remember how the penguins showed up in the exhibit through that inner door after they'd been out on parade?" Mia asked.

They circled the building and found a side door, but no one was hanging around, looking suspicious.

"Should we try inside?" Maddie asked.

"Snow!" Lulu darted toward the door.

Mia had to admit it was pretty hot outside. No one inside the Chill Zone looked suspicious either. A staff member had been throwing fish to the penguins, but now he was packing up his gear.

"Now's the time. Keep your eyes open," Mia said. "Maybe we should go outside?"

Miss Julia wouldn't let them split up, so they decided to wait for five minutes inside, and then watch outside for five minutes. What followed were ten boring minutes. No one inside did anything more suspicious than pushing a nose up against the glass. No one outside did anything more interesting than dropping an ice cream cone on the sidewalk. *Splat.*

"So much for that idea," Mia said, finally admitting defeat.

"Mia, look!" Maddie's voice didn't sound a bit defeated.

But it was only another find for the treasure hunt, this time a polar bear in a rainstorm. He sat in the middle of a fountain with water pouring over the edges of his umbrella. They'd been to the Chill Zone many times, but somehow Mia hadn't noticed him.

"Whoa!" Lulu said.

Mia looked up from her scroll. And blinked. And blinked again. Flamingos, about twelve of them, were high-footing it toward the Chill Zone doors.

"Do you think they're hot and want to cool off too?" Lulu asked.

"What should we do?" Mia asked.

"Hands!" Maddie suggested, holding out hers.

They grabbed hands, roping in Miss Julia, and circled around the flamingos as best they could. A few other people saw what they were doing and joined in to help. Soon, a circle of people held hands, ringing the flamingos in, keeping them in place.

"Now what?" Lulu asked.

As if in answer to her question, a few teenagers in white jackets hurried over. "Thank you!" one said.

They corralled the flamingos into a nearby fenced-in area. One of them radioed for help with returning the flamingos to their regular exhibit.

"Excuse me," Mia said, approaching one of the teens. "I think I know how the animals are being let out."

The teen, a girl with bleached-blond hair, raised an eyebrow at Mia. "Oh, you do, do you?"

"I think someone is letting the animals out during off-feeding hours. That's when you need to watch them."

The girl nodded, mock serious. "Like all the time—whenever we wouldn't normally be keeping an eye on them? Thanks, Sherlock."

"Well, maybe just after feeding time, then. Like these flamingos. When were they last fed?"

"Who knows?"

Mia refused to give up. "Well, maybe it was a little while ago. And afterward, after everyone was gone, Dr. Dolittle came and . . ."

Now, the girl's eyebrow rose even higher than it had the first time. "Dr. Dolittle?"

"No, I mean, that's just what we've been calling him. Obviously, that's not really his name."

"Listen, kid, I have no idea how you found out about our problem, and we're grateful that you rounded up the flamingos for us. Truly. But it's none of your business. Just let us handle things, all right?"

She joined the others, to help herd the flamingos away. Mia felt like one of those cartoon characters who have actual steam come out of their ears. Kid? She hadn't even actually said thank you—just, "We're grateful, but."

"You okay, Mia?" Maddie put her hand on Mia's arm.

When Mia didn't answer, Maddie dropped her hand. Lulu didn't say anything at all. The girls stood there, arms at their sides, three deflated balloons.

"Girls, what do you say we try out Iceberg Float again? Or Alligator Ambush? Maybe this time we can break fifty-three? No?" Miss Julia kept trying. "We all wanted to try Bermuda Triangle. Maybe it's time to head in that direction."

"I guess we could try the Bermuda Triangle . . ." Lulu said, glancing at her sisters.

It wasn't hard to see that Lulu wanted to ride Bermuda Triangle, even though she was trying to maintain her miserable face out of loyalty.

"Bermuda Triangle does sound like fun," Maddie admitted. "Maybe we should take a break on the mystery, Mia? If we stop thinking about it so hard, we might get an idea—you know how that happens sometimes?"

Heat rushed to Mia's cheeks. "We don't need an idea. We have one. The problem is that no one will listen!"

People walking by turned to look, but Mia didn't care. If shouting was what it took for someone to listen to her, then she would shout. From the top of the tallest ride if she had to. She knew she was onto something, and if she had to spend the rest of the day camped outside animal habitats to prove it, she'd do that.

"Is there a way to find out the feeding times?" Mia asked. "I mean, other than by watching, or finding scraps of paper at the exhibits?"

"Maybe there's a schedule at the info desk," Maddie suggested.

"Oh, that makes sense," Mia said. "People like to see the animals when they're being fed, right?"

"Girls . . ." Miss Julia said.

"Come on!" Mia said, starting in that direction.

"I want to go on the Bermuda Triangle ride," Lulu said, digging her heels in too.

"Maybe we can get the feeding schedule and then go on the ride?" Maddie suggested.

Mia breathed deep, trying to control her frustration. "Once we get the feeding schedule, we need to go to see whichever animals are being fed next. Obviously, solving the mystery is the most important thing."

Lulu's expression darkened. "We're supposed to be having fun!"

"Girls, we aren't going to argue," Miss Julia said. "If we need to, we can go home right now."

"No!" all three piped up in unison.

"Let's get the schedule and then go on the ride," Maddie said. "Maybe we can check on some other animals after Bermuda Triangle?"

"Maybe . . ." Lulu said, looking doubtful.

Miss Julia's expression was the exact opposite of doubtful. It was very, very sure. Mia knew that if she pushed it, they'd be going home. Right now. As long as they stayed in the park, even if they had to go on rides to make Lulu happy, she still had a chance of seeing something—anything—and proving those teenagers wrong. She wasn't just a kid with a crazy idea. And

Maddie wasn't the only Glimmer girl able to solve a mystery. Mia would figure this out today, if it was the last thing she did.

TWENTY-TWO

The feeding schedule was posted on a board, but not on any printed schedule they could take with them. Miss Julia took a picture with her phone. The next animal feeding was the sea otters at 1:45. Then, parrots at 2:10 and the walrus at 3:15.

"Dr. Dolittle won't let the flamingos out again today," Mia said. "I don't know that he'd let the sea otters out ever. It seems like a hard exhibit to break into—since it's inside the viewing building. The otters couldn't get very far without people seeing them."

"But maybe there's another door, one that visitors don't use, like there is for the dolphins," Maddie said.

"Maybe . . ." Mia said. "I think we should watch the parrots. They could actually fly away, out of the park, not like the penguins or the flamingos. The parrots are in the most danger, if you think about it."

"Are we going to Bermuda Triangle or not?" Lulu asked.

Miss Julia checked her map. "This way!"

Lulu charged ahead, Miss Julia and Maddie right behind. Mia tried to keep up, but she was also calculating in her head. It was 1:35. If they could line up and ride Bermuda Triangle in 25 or 30 minutes, they might make it to the parrots by feeding time. The barrel ride was near the parrots. Maybe if she reminded Lulu about seeing the seal in the water, she'd be up for looping past the parrots on the way to the ride. It was as good a plan as any.

Maddie held back to walk and talk with Mia. "Maybe the parrots could survive outside the park."

It was almost as though she'd read Mia's mind.

"After Bermuda Triangle, let's do whatever we can to convince Lulu to go past the parrots," Mia said. "I thought we could go there and then ride Barrel Buffoonery again."

"She'd like that," Maddie said. "But she's not going to like sitting and waiting at the parrots, watching for clues."

"She was excited about the mystery when she thought she'd found a clue," Mia said. "Maybe if she finds another one . . ."

"A real one?" Maddie asked.

"Does it matter?" Mia asked.

Maddie shoved her hands into her pockets.

"What?" Mia asked, and when Maddie didn't answer, repeated. "What?!"

"Don't you think . . .?" Then, after trailing off, Maddie said, "Never mind."

"Don't I think what?" Mia insisted.

"You're always the one saying that we shouldn't do the wrong thing, even for the right reasons. And, well . . ."

"You're saying it's the wrong thing to let Lulu feel like she's part of solving the mystery?" Mia asked. "Isn't that what you did in London? Let us feel like we were helping when actually it was just you, all along?"

Maddie's face paled, the way it always did when Mia struck a nerve. "It wasn't just me. We all followed Mr. Hughes."

"My point is, I'm including Lulu," Mia said. "And that's not wrong—what rules would I be breaking?"

"You'd be lying," Maddie said, "if you told her something was a clue and it wasn't."

"How do I know what's a clue and what isn't?" Mia asked. "I didn't think that piece of paper she found was a clue, and maybe it wasn't, but it gave me an idea."

"You're not listening to me," Maddie said.

"Well, you're not listening to me," Mia said, her voice rising.

"What's going on, girls?" Miss Julia asked, slowing to let Mia and Maddie catch up.

"Nothing," they both murmured.

Miss Julia looked from one to the other. "Are we ready for Bermuda Triangle?"

"I want to ride with Lulu," Mia said, ignoring Maddie's sigh.

"Okay," Miss Julia said. "Looks like the line is pretty short for this one."

"Do you think it will be scary?" Lulu asked, as they walked through the triangular-shaped arch.

Inside the entrance hall, twangy piano music played in a minor key. An announcer's voice intoned, "Beware, travelers. Many will enter the Bermuda Triangle, but few will find their way home."

They didn't have long to worry, because they soon found themselves at the front of the line. Mia climbed into the front gondola with Lulu. Maddie and Miss Julia took the next gondola. Fog hissed, circling around the base of the boats. They glided forward, as though they were floating off into the clouds. As they swept around a corner, they found themselves in what appeared to be open, glassy sea. All around them, candelabras rose out of the water and sputtered to life. Mirrors on the walls multiplied each flame, until it seemed as though they were floating on a sea of steam and fire. Next to the Iceberg Float, this was the most beautiful ride Mia had ever seen.

"Whoa," Lulu breathed, her eyes wide.

Mia took her sister's hand, and just in time too, because they had come to the other side of the glassy sea. Now the gondolas increased in speed, heading into the darkness. The sounds of rushing waves and howling wind filled their ears. Lulu held tight to Mia's hand as the boats plummeted down, down, down. Both girls screamed, and Mia squeezed her eyes shut, sure that at any moment they'd be drenched, the way they had been in Scalawag's Splash. But the boat slowed, and glided around a corner, back into another foggy sea.

Now, instead of candlelight, pinpricks of light glowed overhead—starlight dotting the deep-night darkness. They drifted toward a crescent moon.

"Next time, travelers," the voice overhead echoed. "Next time . . ."

No one said anything as they climbed out of the gondolas and headed for the exit.

"It wasn't all that scary," Lulu finally said, as they came out into the sunshine. And then, after a moment, "But it kind of was, wasn't it?"

"Kind of, yeah," Mia agreed.

The ride had almost distracted her from the mystery. Almost. "You know what I saw?" Lulu asked.

"I saw it too!" Maddie said. "*Stay*, written in mist."

"Just as we left the ride!" Lulu agreed.

Miss Julia passed around their scrolls and they added the find to their lists.

"So, I was thinking we should go past the parrots and then to Barrel Buffoonery," Mia said.

"Ooh, and maybe we'll see another seal!" Lulu said.

Mia grinned. The plan had worked.

TWENTY-THREE

The parrot aviary was a net-covered structure, tucked away in a corner of the Southern Atlantic Sea area. A set of double doors, outer and inner, made it so visitors could enter the aviary without letting the birds out.

A biologist gave them each paper cups filled with birdseed when they entered. "You're just in time for a feeding!"

Unlike with the other animals, in the aviary there wasn't any distance between animals and visitors. Parrots swooped down and perched on hands and edges of paper cups, enjoying the feast. Some of the birds were the kind Mia expected, red with orange, blue, and yellow markings. But there were also tropical birds of many other shapes and sizes.

"Are they all parrots?" she asked Miss Julia.

"There are many species of parrots," Miss Julia explained.

Some of the parrots squawked. One landed on Lulu's shoulder and said, "Hello," so loudly that she dumped her cup of seeds on the floor. Maddie offered Lulu the rest of hers, but Lulu was finished with birds. Mia dumped the rest of her seeds out in a line along a rock wall. For one thing, she didn't want any birds landing on her shoulders. Also, she wanted to pay attention and watch for clues.

The parrots had no fear. Anywhere someone had a cup of food, the parrots congregated. Mia watched the outside and inside doors, as people entered and left. It was a pretty safe system. The doors locked with a *click* the moment they closed and stayed that way whenever the other door was open.

"Whatcha drawing?" Lulu asked a boy who was sitting a little way down on the rock wall, watching the feeding too.

He flipped his notebook closed. "Nothing."

"Sorry." Lulu shrugged. "Where are your parents?"

He jumped down off the wall, landing on his feet, and stuffed the notebook into his backpack. Then, Mia recognized him. He was the boy who'd been watching the seals earlier.

"What's his problem?" Lulu asked Mia, as the boy left the exhibit.

"Who knows," Mia said. She didn't have time to worry about some boy. What she needed to do was to find Dr. Dolittle. Time was running out. The biologist packed up her gear and left the exhibit, but no one acted differently after she left. Now that Mia was here, she realized the parrots wouldn't be easy to set free. There was the door locking system, and also, there were so many people everywhere. Someone would see if a person cut a hole in the net or something.

"Barrel ride time?" Lulu asked.

Mia didn't argue. There didn't seem to be any point in waiting around.

They rode the barrel ride twice, and then Miss Julia said, "Okay, girls. Mom's concert is in about three hours, and we only have a little longer in the park. Have you found enough items for your scrolls?"

While Lulu and Maddie counted, Mia racked her brain. There had to be something else, maybe just one more thing that she could do.

"Dancing penguin, singing octopus, queen starfish, stay—written in fog, and a polar bear in a rainstorm. That's five," Maddie said. "We need three more."

"I have six," Lulu said.

"How do you have six?" Maddie asked.

"There was a pirate crab on our walk to Bermuda Triangle," Lulu said. "You were too busy talking to notice."

Maddie frowned. "How do you know it was a pirate crab?"

"It was wearing an eyepatch. He was on a wanted sign posted near the info desk." Maddie and Mia added the pirate crab to their lists. So, they had six, and with Mia's clue, they'd have seven. She knew she should tell them, but she still wanted to win. After they found one more, she'd have made it to eight first, and then she'd tell.

"The walrus," Mia said, with sudden sureness. "What time did you say it was, Miss Julia?"

"3:10," she said.

"They're feeding him at 3:15. If we go now, maybe we'll see something."

"Maybe we'll find another item or two on the way," Maddie added, when Lulu looked ready to argue. "We want the prize, right?"

"I guess," Lulu said.

"Come on!" Mia took off, trying hard to walk when what she really wanted to do was run.

They crossed the Southern Atlantic bridge, but didn't see any plaques or other clues. Across the Arctic bridge, and still nothing. They made it to the walrus just as the biologist was packing up. The walrus had a giant exhibit, a cross between some of the others, with lots of water and also a rocky area. Like the dolphins, a high rock wall bounded his sea pen.

". . . Trouble," Mia heard a man say, to her left. He wore a suit and didn't look like your ordinary park visitor. She edged closer.

"We've interviewed half the staff so far," the other man said. "But no leads. I find it hard to believe that no one has seen anything."

"You think they're covering up for each other?"

"Could be."

"I hate to think it's a park employee—"

At this, he broke off. Mia realized he was staring straight at her. He raised an eyebrow, as if to say, "Did you need something?"

She looked away quickly and hurried back to Miss Julia. So, the park thought Dr. Dolittle was an employee. And they were interviewing everyone. If they went through everyone, they'd have to find Dr. Dolittle sooner or later. And while it wasn't as good as solving the mystery herself, at least she could count on someone being caught soon. Hopefully.

"A book-loving beluga whale!" Maddie said.

Sure enough, there was an iron sculpture of a beluga whale on his back, propping up a book with his fins, near the entrance to the walrus exhibit.

"It's time to go, girls," Miss Julia said, checking her phone again. "We can try to find our last item on the way to the exit, okay?"

"But what if we don't?" Lulu asked.

Now. She should tell them now. But still, Mia kept the golden key a secret. They crossed the bridge, crossed Buccaneer's Island, and crossed the final bridge before the gate. Lulu dragged her feet, looking up and down and all around. Mia sighed. Just because she was disappointed didn't mean she had to make Maddie and Lulu feel that way too.

"It's okay, Lulu," she said. "The golden key was on the submarine."

Lulu spun on her. "You knew that all this time and you didn't tell us?"

"I'm sorry." Mia truly was.

They all wrote this last item onto their scrolls and chose a new prize on their way out. Lulu chose the stuffed sea otter, Mia a stuffed seal, and Maddie the stuffed octopus. Maddie hardly spoke to Mia on the drive back home, which made Mia feel even worse. She hadn't solved the mystery, she hadn't won the game, and she'd let her sisters down.

When they arrived at the bungalow, Miss Julia said, "We're cutting it close. Let's hurry and get dressed. Remember, we need sweaters because we're staying for the fireworks."

TWENTY-FOUR

Mom's concert was at an outdoor amphitheater, and beyond the stage was a beach and then the open sea. Mia was glad Miss Julia had insisted they bring sweaters and blankets. Already, the sea wind was blowing. After all the sunshine, the cool air felt nice, but later it was sure to be cold.

Miss Julia led the girls to their seats. Music played over the loudspeakers, but the band hadn't taken the stage yet. Mom had chosen seats in the first row of the first balcony for the girls, rather than right up next to the stage. That way, they'd have a perfect viewing location for the fireworks after the show.

Fireworks and a concert, Mia told herself. *Have fun. Let the mystery go.*

A mystery wouldn't be a mystery if it were simple to solve. Just because she hadn't figured out who Dr. Dolittle was, didn't mean she shouldn't have tried. Maybe she'd solve the next one.

Mia shifted in her seat. The trouble was, no matter what she told herself, nothing made the failure any easier to accept. Maddie had solved her mystery. Mia hadn't solved hers. On top of that, Mia could feel Maddie watching her, judging her for not telling about the key sooner.

"Which was your favorite ride?" Lulu asked. "Bermuda Triangle, Barrel Buffoonery, or the Iceberg Float?"

"What about Alligator Ambush?" Mia asked.

Lulu raised an eyebrow. "That was your favorite?"

"It might have been if we had won," Mia said. "I liked High Jinks too."

"Those pirates were funny," Lulu agreed. "My favorite ride was the Bermuda Triangle, though."

"Smile, girls!" Miss Julia said, snapping a photo of Lulu and Mia on one side of her, and then Maddie on the other. "Okay, so if you could invent any ride, what would it be like?"

Lulu didn't have to think about it. "Scary and fast."

"Not me," Maddie said. "I'd want to make one that felt magical, like the Iceberg Float, or like Bermuda Triangle."

Usually, this was just the kind of question Mia would love. Ideas would pop to mind and she'd have a whole ride figured out, maybe even a whole amusement park. Not tonight.

"So, my ride would be in the dark," Lulu began. "And it would be scary because you'd hear the sound of something . . . maybe a rumbling sound. Ooh, or maybe thunder, and then lightning would flash."

"Doesn't lightning come first?" Maddie asked.

"Usually," Miss Julia agreed.

"Well, in my ride, the thunder would come first. And then . . . *wham!* There would be this blinding flash of lightning. And then, *whoosh!*" Lulu flung her arm to demonstrate, almost knocking into a woman in the row behind them. "Oops, sorry!"

Just then, everyone started cheering and clapping. The band had taken the stage. Mom entered, beaming at the crowd as the band struck up her first song. Music poured into the crowd, flowing in and around Mia. At first, her questions and frustration beat in counterpoint to the music, but after one song, and then another, the beat worked its way inside. She felt herself letting go. Mia had heard all the words to all Mom's songs, but still, sometimes certain words stood out. A phrase might catch Mia's ear in an unexpected way.

"He's got the whole world in his hands," Mom sang, a line she'd woven into the lyrics, echoing back to the Sunday school song. The whole world. The dolphins and the seals and the penguins—even Dr. Dolittle. And that meant God had Mia, too, in his hands.

"Help me," Mia whispered, the only prayer she could come up with. Help her what? Solve the mystery? Get over the mystery? Talk to Maddie? Figure out why right and wrong felt so tangled up, so impossible to understand? God had her in his hands. No matter how confused she was, she knew this was also true. Not just because Mom had just sung it, or because she'd heard

it so many times in Sunday school. She knew it because all her life, she'd seen it was true, over and over. She and Mom would pray about a difficult situation, and even when it seemed it would never—could never—work out, somehow it would.

There was the time when she hadn't made the soccer team. She'd felt just as stormy inside as she felt now, but after they'd prayed—and prayed—eventually, she'd started feeling a little better. And that year her school had put on the play *Alice in Wonderland*. Mia had gotten to play Alice, something she couldn't have done if she'd been too busy playing soccer. Or there was the time Leah Jenkins had blamed Mia for telling one of her secrets. No matter what Mia said, Leah wouldn't believe her. It took two weeks of praying before Leah finally started talking to Mia again. It had taken even longer before they were the kind of friends they'd been before. But then, late in spring, Leah had told Mia another secret, and Mia knew that Leah trusted her again. As long as Mia had insisted on being right, Leah couldn't let it go. But praying had worked when nothing else had. So, maybe praying would work now.

Mom and the band struck a chord, and it was time for the last song—the girls' song. Mia, Lulu, Miss Julia, and Maddie all held hands and swayed to the music. As the last notes faded, *boom*! Fireworks lit up the night. Red and blue and then the silver ones that burst in hundreds of sparks and fell like water spilling out of the sky. Flash after flash, they rumbled in Mia's chest, shaking loose the last of her disappointment. She didn't know how she'd let the mystery go, but she would. She glanced over at Maddie. And as soon as she found the right moment, she'd apologize to her sister, even if she wasn't the only one who'd done things wrong.

The fireworks finale began, with color layering over color, flash after flash until finally the sky went dark.

TWENTY-FIVE

"Put on your pjs girls," Miss Julia said. "Then we can go out on the beach to watch the stars until Mom and Dad come home."

When Mia walked out onto the beach, the breeze was soft against her cheeks. Her toes sunk gently into the still-cooling sand with each step. *Shhh*, the night seemed to say. *Peace*. Mia tried to settle into the quiet, but inside, she felt more like the sizzle and pop of the fireworks than the steady *hushhh-hushhh* of the rolling waves. Her list of things to do played on auto-repeat in her mind. Apologize to Maddie. Let go of swimming with the dolphins. Leave the park's mystery for someone else to solve.

She wrapped her blanket around her body, sat, and then slowly lay back so she could see the stars. If she wasn't making them into star pictures, they looked almost exactly like one another. Was this the way humans looked when God watched them from heaven? Like so many identical dots of light? Or did God see each person—Mia with her glasses and blond hair and painted pink toenails? From a long, long way away, maybe the details didn't matter.

No. In the quiet, it was as though the word was delivered directly to Mia, right into her mind and heart.

No. The details did matter, and not only the outside ones, like glasses, but the inside ones too. Details such as her fireworks-filled heart and her need to make things right with Maddie. Not just-for-now right, but truly right.

The screen door opened again, and Maddie and Lulu came out. "Where are you, Mia?" Lulu whispered, and then giggled, "Oops!" as she tripped over Mia in the dark.

"Found me," Mia said, brushing sand out of her face.

Her sisters lay on either side of her, wrapped up in their blankets too. "See any pictures?" Maddie asked Mia.

"Not yet," Mia answered, and then catching a tiny flash out of the corner of her eye, turned to Lulu. "What's that?"

"Nothing," Lulu said, closing her hand into a fist, and then stuffing her arm back into her blanket.

"No, really, what was it?" Mia asked, sitting up.

"Nothing," Lulu said, sounding defensive now.

"Let her be," Maddie said. "It's probably just a shell or something."

"Something flashed in her hand," Mia said. "Like something glow in the dark or . . . Come on, Lulu, what is it?"

"I. Told. You." Lulu said, each word coming out as though it were a sentence of its own. "I don't have anything."

Mia considered tickling her sister until she gave her secret up, but as the screen door opened again and Miss Julia came outside, she decided against it. If Lulu's secret was no big deal, it was no big deal. If it was a big deal, and Mia forced her to spill the beans, she'd definitely get in trouble. Mia lay back. Immediately, she sat up again with a jolt.

"Whoa, what?" Maddie said. "What's wrong, Mia?"

"Lulu's secret," Mia said.

"I told you, I don't . . ." Lulu insisted, sitting up too.

"No, no," Mia said. "Remember the boy today, the boy with the backpack? We saw him by the parrots. And Lulu wanted to know what he was writing in his notebook. He slammed it shut and stuffed it into his backpack."

"Yeah, so?" Maddie said. "What does that have to do with Lulu's secret?"

"Nothing," Mia said, frustrated that her sisters weren't catching up more quickly. "He acted like that, defensive, because he had a secret, an important secret."

"What secret?" Lulu wanted to know.

"I just heard your parents drive in," Miss Julia said. "They'll be out in a second, I'm sure."

The unanswered question hung in the air, and Mia wasn't sure whether to answer it now with Miss Julia here. She'd promised to let the mystery go, so bringing it up right now wouldn't be popular, she was sure.

"Girls!" Mom's voice rang out across the sand as she and Dad came through the screen door. "What did you think of those fireworks?"

"Awesome," said Maddie.

"Double awesome," said Lulu.

"Who wants to dip their toes in the ocean with me?" Dad asked.

"Me!" Lulu and Maddie answered, sitting up to roll up their pj pants.

They left their blankets behind and followed Dad toward the waves. Miss Julia went too, snapping nighttime pics with her cell phone.

TWENTY-SIX

And how about you?" Mom asked, sitting down next to Mia on Maddie's blanket. "Did you think the fireworks were awesome?"

"Mom, can I please go back to the park tomorrow?" Mia asked.

"What's this?" Mom asked, and even in the dim starlight, Mia could see her frown of concern. "You went yesterday and today . . . I'd think that would be enough, Mia. What's going on?"

"I figured out . . ." Mia stopped herself, realizing she was going to have to make this good to convince Mom. "So you know I heard about that problem at the park."

"Yes," Mom said.

"And then, Lulu found that scrap of paper that turned out to be a clue."

"Was it?"

"Yes, because we realized the animals were escaping their habitats just after their feeding times. So, we knew when we should be watching. But we didn't see anyone letting the animals out today."

"That's a good thing, right?" Mom asked.

"Well, someone let the flamingos out," Mia said. "But we didn't see them do it. We helped round them up, though. We held hands and stood in a circle around them until the biologists came."

"Sounds like you girls were helpful today," Mom said.

"But we didn't catch Dr. Dolittle," Mia said.

"Dr. who?" Mom asked.

"That's what we've been calling him," Mia said. "Or her. Actually him. Because now I know who he is."

"I'm sorry, I don't think I understand," Mom said. "You know who has been letting out the animals?"

"We saw him today," Mia said, feeling exasperated.

"But you said you didn't see him?" Mom said, sounding more than a little frustrated herself.

"We didn't know we saw him. But tonight, Lulu had something in her hand, something secret. She tried to hide it, and I knew. I just knew. See, there was this boy, and he was writing in a notebook. Lulu asked him what he was doing and he acted all defensive and walked away. And his notebook, it was the same size paper as the scrap Lulu found in the Chill Zone."

"A boy?" Mom asked. "Mia, this sounds like a lot of assumptions. I don't think a boy could let out the animals. Wouldn't his parents notice?"

"That's the thing. His parents weren't with him, not all day. I saw him this morning and later this afternoon, and he was always alone."

"Well . . ." Mom said. "That may be, but this is still a lot of guesses, Mia. Plus, whatever's happening in the park isn't our concern."

"But I know who's letting the animals out," Mia insisted. "I have to go tell them."

"I understand you feel like you need to," Mom said. "But solving this problem is not your responsibility. We'd need more proof than a boy acting secretive."

"Solving the mystery in London wasn't Maddie's responsibility either, but look what she did."

"Maddie broke a lot of rules in London too," Mom said. "I'm afraid that solving the mystery in London— even though it was a good thing to have helped—" she added, speaking right over Mia's objection. "I think solving the mystery made you girls extra sensitive to problems. Not every problem is ours to fix, you know. And I'm concerned that this has become a bit of a competition. Do you feel you need to solve a mystery just because Maddie did?"

This question was a little too close for comfort. "Why do you treat Maddie and me differently? When I try to do something good, I'm being competitive. And when she does the same kind of thing, it's courageous. That's not fair."

"Mia . . ." Mom started.

"You and Dad and Miss Julia all treated Maddie like she was so special because she found the art thief. Sure, she didn't get to watch movies on the flight here, but mostly, you're treating her like a hero. And now, I'm doing the same thing, and you're telling me I shouldn't."

"I'm not saying you shouldn't stand up for what you think is right," Mom said. "And I don't mean to treat you and Maddie differently. You are both special in your own ways, and I have unique relationships with each of you. You know how much we all wanted Maddie to be brave. Think about how much more willing she is now to sing with us on stage, for instance. Maybe that's because she surprised herself with her own courage when she found the thief in London. I'm not proud of Maddie for sneaking out, but I am proud of the way she's growing . . . and I know you're proud of her for that too."

"It's wrong to break rules," Mia said.

"It is," Mom agreed.

"So how come sometimes it's also right?" Mia asked. "It used to be that right was right and wrong was wrong, but now I don't know what to think. Or what to do."

Mom put an arm around Mia and pulled her close. "Sweet, sweet Mia."

Mia relaxed into the hug, knowing that Mom hadn't heard only the question, but also the frustration beneath it. Finally, finally, she'd been heard. And maybe that was enough.

Mom squeezed Mia one more time and then drew a line in the sand with her finger. "Sometimes right and wrong are as simple as this line in the sand. Cruelty, for instance, is always wrong. Being kind, sparkling and shining the way my Glimmer girls do, that's right. But some things—such as speaking up or waiting, or getting involved or not—those things can't be easily put on one side of the line or the other. Each situation is unique, the way each of you girls are unique."

"So how are we supposed to know what to do?"

"Sometimes the right thing to do is very clear. God puts something on our hearts and we know we just have to follow through. Other times, it's hard to know."

"I need to go back to the park, Mom. I need to tell them about the boy."

"I understand you feel that way," Mom said. "But our flight is tomorrow. We just don't have time for another visit to the park. We'll have to pray that if it is this boy you saw, the park officials will discover him very soon."

"You don't believe me," Mia said. "If you did, you'd let me go."

"Mia, I did let you go to the park again today. But you promised that if the mystery didn't get solved today, you'd let it go."

Mia scooped up a handful of sand and let it pour through her fingers. It was true, she had agreed to let it go. What else was she supposed to say? The list was still there, circling through her mind. Apologize to Maddie. Let go of swimming with the dolphins. Leave the park's mystery for someone else to solve. She didn't want to do any of these things.

"How about we sleep on it," Mom said. "We're all tired. And if we need to, we can talk again tomorrow. Okay?"

Mia breathed in the night air, and then blew it out slowly. "Okay. Deal."

Mom squeezed her tight again before standing to call to the others. "Bedtime for the Glimmer family."

TWENTY-SEVEN

One seashell each," Mom said as she passed by their room to drop off shoes and other items that had been strewn across the beach house.

"But I have a bunch of baby ones," Lulu said. "How many baby seashells equal a big one?"

"I'll help them figure it out," Miss Julia jumped in. "I just finished packing."

"Oh, thank you, Julia," Mom said. "Jack and I are far from finished."

"Not a problem." Miss Julia came into the girls' room and surveyed the mess. "Hmm . . . Maybe I spoke too soon?"

"I can't fit my stuff in my bag," Maddie said.

"My tiara won't fit," Lulu said.

"Everything fit when we packed in the first place," Mia complained.

"But then you added your stuffed animals from the park, and your London sightseeing purchases. And what are these?" Miss Julia fished a handful of rocks out of Lulu's bag.

"Rocks," Lulu said.

"I can see that," Miss Julia said, clearly trying not to laugh. "And why are you packing a handful of rocks, Lulu?"

"They're ocean rocks," Lulu said. "All different colors. Purple and green and even red. Look at that one."

Mia checked. How had Lulu found a red rock? Turned out the rock was actually gray with only the tiniest tinge of red.

"It looked redder when it was wet," Lulu insisted.

"So, can we at least leave the red one behind?" Miss Julia asked. "As it is, it will take one of those strong men from the circus to lift your bag into the airplane bin."

Mia stuffed the last few items into her suitcase and wrestled it closed. The clock read 8:12. The park opened at 9:00. Mom had said no last night, but she'd also said they could talk about it again today. One last chance.

"Be right back," she said to the others and hurried to her parents' room.

Mom and Dad were in constant motion, collecting items, sorting them, folding them, finding the right bag. Mia knew she'd have to ask her question with extreme caution.

"Mom?" she started.

"Mmm?" Mom tucked her concert heels into the suitcase.

"You know how you said we could talk about going back to the park today?"

"Mia . . ." Dad said.

"Not to ride rides or anything, and just for a minute," Mia rushed on. "I figured out who has been letting the animals out of their habitats. And you want the animals to be safe, don't you?"

Dad took in the half-finished packing. "We have plenty to do without stuffing another park trip into our day."

"Can just Mom and I go then?" Mia asked. "Our flight isn't until 3:00, and that's plenty of time. Please, Mom?"

Mom scooted a pile of clothing out of the way and made room for Mia on the bed. "Close the door, will you, Mia?"

Mia did, a sense of dread growing. She took her time crossing the room to join Mom on the bed.

"I've been thinking about what you asked last night," Mom said. "You asked how to know if something is right or wrong. A lot of times, knowing has to do with our reasons for our actions. Sometimes we pray for God's help, and he says no even though we're asking for something he'd want for us. When that happens, it's often because we're asking for the wrong reasons."

Mia nodded, not sure where this was headed. Was Mom about to say yes—that she could go to the park?

"I need to ask you a question, and I want you to think about it, and then answer me truthfully."

"Okay." Mia held her breath. Maybe . . . maybe . . .

"Do you think you're competing with Maddie? Are you set on finding this boy because Maddie solved a mystery and you want to do the same?"

Mia's shoulders sagged. So, no. She wouldn't be going to the park today. She didn't have to think for more than a few seconds to know that she was competing with Maddie. Still, she couldn't lie. Lying would definitely be the wrong thing to do. She couldn't make lying right by then doing a right thing and solving the mystery.

She blew out the breath she was holding. "Yes. It's partly because of Maddie. If she can solve a mystery, I know I can solve one too."

Mia wanted to say, "But . . ." and include all the other reasons she wanted to solve the mystery. Though Mom was right. If one of her reasons—the biggest one—was wrong, the other reasons didn't matter.

Mom looked thoughtfully at Dad, who nodded, and then said, "You said partly. What are the other reasons?"

"The animals in the park are all injured or need help, or they can't live on their own in the wild. If the wrong animals actually escape the park, they could die. And if the boy is the one letting them out, he can't be doing it for money or anything like that. He's just a kid. So, maybe he doesn't understand. I think I can help—I want to help. I'm afraid we'll go home and I'll hear that he let an animal out and it got hurt or . . . died. I think I can stop that from happening. At least, I want to try."

"Now that," Dad said, "is what I'd call a right reason."

"I'm proud of you," Mom put her hand on Mia's knee. "You could have been dishonest or claimed that your feelings about Maddie didn't matter. But you told us the truth, when I know telling the truth wasn't easy. And like Dad said, you do have a heartfelt, very right reason too."

Hope bloomed inside Mia, making it hard to sit still. "So does that mean we can go?"

Mom checked the clock, and then asked Dad, "Can you finish this up? We can plan to meet at the airport at two. Maybe you could take the other girls for lunch and a treat?"

"I think that can be arranged," Dad said.

"So yes?" Mia asked, eyes wide.

Mom winked. "Yes."

Mia jumped off the bed, whooping. She hugged Mom and Dad and then Mom again. "Thank you, thank you, thank you!"

TWENTY-EIGHT

They arrived at the park just as the attendants opened the front gates. As soon as they were through, Mia paused, scanning the various paths. On the way to the park, she'd considered her options. How could she find the boy quickly? He'd already let out the penguins and flamingos in the last few days, so maybe he'd go for a different exhibit. Yesterday, she'd seen him watching the seals and the parrots. Since the seals were already free—at least the ones he'd been watching were free—she didn't think she needed to worry about them. She'd been sure yesterday that no one could get away with letting the parrots out without anyone seeing. But sometimes kids got away with things that adults couldn't. He wasn't too much older than she was, and if someone saw him sneaking around the back of the aviary, they'd think he was just a kid messing around, not someone making real trouble. Maybe early in the morning he'd be able to cut a hole in the net without being caught.

"I think we should go to the parrots," she told Mom. "But let's see what time they get fed over at the info desk."

Morning feeding time for the parrots was 9:45. Right now, it was 9:15, so it would be a bit of a wait.

Mia led the way to the parrots. When they got there, she searched the aviary inside and out. No boy with a backpack. Also, there wasn't much of a crowd. If they camped out, the boy might see and recognize her. If she scared him away, he might not show his face at all today, and then her last chance would really and truly be over.

"I suppose we should make the rounds," Mia said.

"Sure," Mom said. "Don't see him?"

"Nope," Mia said.

"Remember . . ." Mom began.

"I know, we might not find him and I have to be okay with that." Mom nudged Mia with her shoulder, smiling.

"Love you, Mia."

"You too, Mom," Mia said.

Captain Swashbuckler's Adventure Park felt bigger than ever today. Every single family seemed to want to go the opposite way that Mia wanted to go. It was like being a fish swimming upstream in a strong current. First, they made their way to the Chill Zone. No backpack boy, inside or outside the exhibit. Rather than heading across Buccaneer's Island, they circled the park counterclockwise, past the flamingos—no boy— and on toward the sea otter exhibit. Mia walked around as far around the back of the building as the walkway allowed. Still, she didn't see any entrance other than a chained and padlocked fence. The only backstage access to the otters had to be on the other side.

"Can I help you?" a park employee asked. Clearly, they weren't supposed to be poking around back here.

"Excuse us," Mom said. "We're not in the right place, are we?"

"If you're looking for the entrance to the otters, it's around this way," the man said.

He led them toward a well-traveled path in front of the building and watched until they went inside. The sea otters were playing, as usual, and no one was entering or exiting through the side doors. Not that Mia had expected anyone to be letting otters out into the public area. No backpack boy here either.

Now that they weren't stopping to ride rides, Mia realized how exhausting it was to walk and walk and walk around the giant park. But she could hardly give up now. The boy had to be somewhere, and she fully planned to find him.

Around the top of the park, they crossed into the Arctic Sea area. Mia checked the walrus exhibit.

"He had a severe infection when he beached," Mom said, reading the plaque. "And it kept recurring, until they determined he'd have to remain on small amounts of medication for the rest of his life."

"He weighs 3,200 pounds," Mia read. "Umm . . . Dr. Dolittle wouldn't let him out, would he? Anyway, I don't see the boy anywhere." Mia scanned the crowd for red backpacks. "It's strange now, calling the kid Dr. Dolittle, but I don't know what else to call him."

"Ready to move on?" Mom asked.

"Yes." Mia tried to stay optimistic, but she was starting to worry. She'd been sure they'd have spotted the boy by now. They'd walked through more than half of the park.

"The Northern Atlantic Sea area is ahead," Mia said. "Dolphins and seals. Probably, he won't be there either, but you should see the seals since you didn't see them when you came. Did you know they were here before the park was built?"

"And they stuck around?" Mom asked.

"Their cove is pretty special," Mia said. "The scientist we talked to said that they are safe there from predators, like sharks. And I think they like showing off for the people, at least that's what it seemed like to me."

"Maybe so," Mom said. "Lead the way!"

TWENTY-NINE

The seals barked just as loudly as they had yesterday. Mia and Mom leaned against the rail to watch them splash off their rocks into the water. The seals rolled around in the waves, and then climbed back out. While they watched, something made Mia turn and look at the dolphin and seal hospital.

"Mom, that's him!" Mia said, grabbing Mom's arm.

He wore his red backpack again, and like yesterday, he was alone.

"Watch out!" Mia said, as the boy glanced over his shoulder to see if anyone was watching.

Both she and Mom whipped their heads back toward the seals. After counting to twenty, Mia peeked again. He must not have seen them. Now, he had something white in his hand, something white and small, the size of a key card. He approached the door again.

"See?" Mia said to Mom.

Mom took out her phone and snapped a picture, but looked uncertain as she studied it. "I'm not sure."

Something must have spooked the boy, because just then, he bolted away from the door. He disappeared into the park.

"Now what?" Mia asked.

"He did have a key card," Mom said. "Doesn't it make sense that he's maybe a son of one of the scientists?"

"Then why would he run away?" Mia asked. "If he had a key card that worked, and that belonged to him, wouldn't he simply unlock the door and go inside?"

"I don't know . . ." Mom said.

"Mom, we have proof. We have to go tell someone. We have to."

"To be honest, Mia, I'm regretting coming to the park today. I'm afraid you're going to be disappointed. What if we're about to lead the park officials on a wild-goose chase?"

"What if it isn't a wild-goose chase?"

Mom looked at the picture once more. "I suppose we should go find someone to talk to. You said you saw a scientist over by those doors yesterday?"

"Yes, but no one is there now. Maybe we should go to the info desk?"

"That's probably the thing to do," Mom agreed.

Mia didn't mind the ache in her feet, now that they were on their way to do something, to finally share her theory. Now that she'd seen him in front of the dolphin and seal hospital, she was even more determined. If he messed with the injured dolphins or seals, who knew what would happen. She had to stop him before he made a mistake that couldn't be fixed.

The info desk attendant wore a pirate costume, complete with an eye patch and a red bandana to cover her salt-and-pepper gray braids.

"Ahoy there," she called as they approached. "How might I help ye?"

Mia waited until they'd closed the distance. Then, she said, "Someone's letting the animals out of their habitats. We think we know who."

"Excuse me?" the woman asked, completely dropping her pirate persona.

Mia repeated herself. The woman glanced at Mom, who said, "We should probably talk to a park official."

"Right," said the woman, and thinking this through, repeated, "Right. Just a moment."

She picked up her phone, dialed a number, and explained that a girl had important information to share.

"Right," she said yet again as she hung up. "Please wait on this bench, and Gabrielle Yates, head of park security, will be with you shortly."

Gabrielle Yates looked like an Olympic athlete, maybe a runner. Mia had no idea how old she was; she could be thirty or fifty, Mia wouldn't have been able to tell the difference. Gabrielle's face was mostly unlined, but had sharp angles, particularly at her cheekbones. She walked at a brisk pace, and once at the bench, she held out her hand to shake their hands. Mia liked Gabrielle immediately, noticing that she shook her hand first, and then Mom's.

"It's nice to meet you, Mia. Gloria. Follow me to my office?" Gabrielle suggested.

"Thank you," Mom said.

Gabrielle led them to an office building on the edge of the Antarctic Ocean area. Inside, accent walls were blue and green, and the decor was similar to the rest of the park. Large frames hung on the walls, featuring photos of various animals being released into the sea.

"Success stories," Gabrielle said, motioning to the photos. "We love being a destination for families—for fun and for education—but the mission closest to our hearts is saving the animals and releasing them back into the wild."

"Hey there, Sara," she said, passing by a woman at a wide reception desk. Once inside the suite of offices, she held open the door for Mia and Mom. "Come on inside."

There was a sitting area across from the desk. Mia and Mom sat on the couch, and Gabrielle sat in a wing-backed chair next to them.

"Tell me everything," Gabrielle said to Mia.

THIRTY

I t all started when we were backstage to see the dolphins," Mia said. "I went to the restroom, and when I
came back out into the hallway, I overheard a couple of
teenagers talking. They said that someone was letting
the animals out of their habitats."

Gabrielle nodded seriously. "It's been happening
off and on all summer, but in the past few weeks, we've
had an incident almost every day. We're baffled. For
starters, how could anyone with poor intentions enter
the park so often without catching the attention of our
front gate staff?"

"I told my sisters what I'd heard, and we started
looking for clues," Mia said.

"We were recently in London, and my girls stumbled
across a mystery that they ended up solving," Mom
explained. "I'm afraid they've caught the detective bug."

"We didn't find any real clues on Thursday," Mia
said. "But then I begged Mom and Dad and they let us
come back yesterday with our nanny, Miss Julia. That's
when we came up with the idea that maybe this person—" She just stopped herself from calling him Dr.
Dolittle. She didn't want to explain their thief's code
name to Gabrielle. "Maybe he was letting the animals
out immediately after feeding times. On Thursday, in

the Chill Zone, my sister found a scrap of paper with feeding times written on it. No one thought it was a clue. Not then. But after we thought about it, we realized maybe it was."

"Maybe Gabrielle doesn't need quite so much of the story," Mom suggested.

"No, it's all right," Gabrielle said. "It's an interesting theory. Why did you think he was letting animals out after feeding time?"

"He could watch the biologists leave after their shifts were over. Then, he'd know the animals were on their own for a while."

Gabrielle went to her desk, pulled out a file folder, and flipped through pages before coming back to join them. "The timing actually checks out. That could be exactly what he—or she—is doing."

"He. It's a boy," Mia said. "See, we saw this kid making notes in a notebook, and he acted all . . . shifty when my sister talked to him. I didn't notice then. Well, actually I just didn't pay enough attention. But last night, my little sister had something in her hands, something secret. When I asked her about it, she got all secretive—just like he had—and then I knew."

"That's why you think it's this boy? Because he was acting secretive?" Gabrielle's forehead creased.

"I wasn't sure what to think either," Mom said. "Certainly, we needed more proof. So we came back today."

"And we saw him with a key card over by the dolphin and seal hospital. Maybe he was about to break in, I don't know. But something spooked him and he ran off. Mom took his picture."

"Can I see?" Gabrielle asked. Mom handed over her phone.

"But that's . . ." Gabrielle said, her frown lines deepening. "He shouldn't have a key card. What is he doing?"

She rose from her chair again and went to her phone. "Tim, can you come in here?" Almost instantly, a man wearing a black suit and round glasses walked through the door.

"What is it?"

Gabrielle showed him the picture. "This girl seems to think Jackson is the one letting animals out of their habitats."

The man—Tim, she'd called him—blinked rapidly, reminding Mia of a surprised owl. "But Jackson, he's completely nuts about the animals. I mean, he wouldn't, he couldn't . . ." The man's voice trailed off.

Mia got the impression that mental pieces were falling into place, fitting together in a brand-new way, a way he hadn't considered until this moment.

"Do you think it's possible?" he asked Gabrielle.

"If it's Jackson," Gabrielle said, "it's not out of malice, that's for sure."

"I've been trying to explain to him," Tim said. "We've been talking about this for years, and he never seems to understand . . . Gaby, what should we do?"

"Why don't you let me talk to him first," she said. "He trusts me, and maybe he'll tell me the truth. First, we need to see if this is actually what has been happening. If it is, then we can decide what to do."

Tim blinked again, looking dazed. "Right. Of course. I'll send Sara to round him up."

Gabrielle sat again. "I'd like you to stay, Mia. Jackson, as you may have guessed, is Tim's son. Tim is the park director. Jackson, as you'll probably see, is passionate about the animals. He's a full-steam animal rights activist. He's come with us for every animal release since he was three years old—that's been about ten years now. We've been looking for someone who might mean the animals harm, someone who would want to steal and sell the animals or someone who wanted to play pranks on the park authorities. We hadn't considered that someone who loved the animals would . . . In any case, we'll see."

Soon, Jackson came through the door, his arms crossed over his chest. "What?" he asked, and then when he spotted Mia on the couch, "What's she doing here?"

"Jackson, this is Mia and her mom, Gloria. Have a seat." Gabrielle motioned for the chair opposite.

"I'd rather stand," he said, glowering at Mia.

"Something serious has been going on, Jackson," Gabrielle said. "And Mia thinks you might be involved. And I think you may be involved too. I want you to understand, we're just trying to get to the bottom of things, all right? We need for you to tell us the truth."

"Where's my dad?" Jackson asked.

"In his office. For now, this is between you and me," Gabrielle said.

"Hmph," was all Jackson had to say in reply.

THIRTY-ONE

Gabrielle showed Jackson the picture on Mom's phone. "Where did you get this key card, Jackson? And why were you using it in an area you're not authorized to be?"

"I didn't go into that building." Jackson shrugged. "I couldn't get in."

"But you were trying to get in," Gabrielle prodded. "Why?"

Jackson shrugged again. "I found the key card and thought it might work. I wanted to see the seals. I heard that one of them is ready for release."

"Soon, yes," Gabrielle said. "But we have to get approval first, of course."

Jackson shrugged a third time, but Mia got the impression that Jackson wasn't really the shrugging sort of kid. His eyes sparked and fire lurked just under the nonchalant attitude.

"You understand why we need approval, don't you, Jackson?" Gabrielle asked, surprising Mia with this sideways question.

Mia wanted to blurt out her accusation rather than dance around the issue. Mom put her hand on Mia's knee, warning her to wait. Mia shifted uncomfortably, wondering how Mom so often seemed to know what she was about to do.

"Sure, I understand that there's red tape," Jackson said.

"Not red tape," Gabrielle said. "We have to ensure that the animals are ready to survive on their own in the wild."

"They're wild animals," Jackson said, his patience beginning to crack. "Wild. Would you like to be locked up in a cage your whole life?"

"No, I wouldn't," Gabrielle said calmly. "But I'm not an injured dolphin or a sea otter who's too used to humans for her own safety."

"If they could speak for themselves, they'd tell you they wanted to be free," Jackson said. "You can see it in their eyes. Maybe they wouldn't survive forever in the wild, but why not give them a year of freedom rather than a long, boring life in a cage?"

"An injured dolphin will hardly last a month in open sea, let alone a year," Gabrielle said. "You know our animals not only help educate people so that more sea life can stay wild, but they also help to rehabilitate other injured animals. The resident animals make it possible for at least some of our visitors to return to a wild, free life."

"If they wanted to be teachers, you'd think they would have said so," Jackson said.

"Letting animals out of their habitats isn't anything to joke about, Jackson," Gabrielle said. "What if one of those penguins had climbed out of the park and was loose on a San Diego beach? What if a park visitor stepped on a sea turtle because he didn't expect to find one outside the habitat?"

"None of those things happened," Jackson said.

"But you were the one who let the animals out, weren't you?" Gabrielle asked. Jackson stared at her and then down at his feet.

Mia finally understood. Gabrielle had pulled the truth out of Jackson without ever accusing him. He'd never had reason to be defensive or shout or make excuses. Well, he'd made excuses, but not as a cover-up for what he'd done.

As she watched Jackson stare at his shoes and listened to the silence that filled the room, a small voice inside her head whispered, *You did it*. After everything, she had solved the mystery. She'd been right about Jackson.

Convincing Mom to come back to the park had been worth it. All the clue-searching and thinking and puzzling out, it had all been worth it.

"All right, Jackson," Gabrielle said. "I'd like for you to wait outside with Sara, and I'll finish up with Mia and her mom."

Jackson trudged out of the office, and Mia wondered whether he'd walk right past Sara's desk. Gabrielle poked her head out and called, "Sara, will you hang out with Jackson for a minute? I'll be with you both shortly."

"That was amazing," Mia said, as Gabrielle came back into the room. "How did you know just what to ask him? You should be a lawyer."

"Mia, thank you," Gabriella said. "Without your insight, it would have taken us a long time to figure out that Jackson was the one behind this situation. From what I heard today, I'm guessing he might have even taken matters into his own hands and tried to release a seal from the sea pens. That wouldn't have been anywhere near as easy to solve as rounding up a few escaped penguins. We're so grateful to you for your help."

Heat rushed to Mia's cheeks, and the glow of happiness that had begun when Jackson admitted his guilt—by not saying anything at all—spread through her.

"We want to give your family lifetime passes to the park, of course," Gabrielle said. "And is there anything else you'd like, anything at all we can give you as a thank you?"

"I'm just happy that the animals are safe," Mia said, meaning it. "I had a dream where one of the dolphins had gotten loose. He looked me in the eyes, his scared, scared eyes looking right into mine, and I had to figure out what was happening. I had to do whatever I could to help keep them safe."

"Sounds like you've got the beginnings of a marine biologist here," Gabrielle said to Mom. "Oh! Mia, didn't you say that you had wanted to swim with the dolphins?"

"Yes, before I understood that having strangers in the water with them wouldn't be healthy for them," Mia said.

"In general, that's true," Gabrielle said. "Particularly for the dolphins that will eventually go back out to sea. But our two full-time resident dolphins, the ones who can never go back to the wild, sometimes do provide educational dolphin encounters. Scientists need to interact with dolphins to learn more about them, so they can learn to work with injured animals. We don't sell tickets for people to swim with our dolphins, but I'm sure in this special case, we could arrange an in-water visit. Would you like that?"

Mia looked up at Mom with big, hopeful eyes. "I didn't wear my swimming suit!"

Mom laughed. "I suppose we could buy you a swimming suit on Buccaneer's Island, don't you think?"

"Thank you! Wow." Mia said to Gabrielle, and then as laughter bubbled out of her, she said again. "Thank you!"

"Thank you, Mia. Everyone on staff, and the animals too, can't thank you enough for your help."

"Could my . . ." Mia started, and then was afraid to finish her question. No, she had to ask. She'd solved the mystery, but Maddie and Lulu had definitely helped. "My sisters. Could they come too?"

"Three may be too many," Gabrielle said. "But I bet they could come and watch if you'd like them to."

Gabrielle traded with Sara, taking Jackson back into her office and leaving Mia and Mom at the reception desk to sort out details for park passes and to set up the dolphin swim. Mia started to get nervous when it seemed there wouldn't be time to set up the swim and make their plane in time. Finally, they settled on a 12:45 swim.

Mom called Dad and asked him to bring the girls and Miss Julia to the park whenever he could. "There will be passes waiting for you at the front desk."

"All set?" Sara asked.

"All set," Mia said.

THIRTY-TWO

After they'd chosen a swimsuit, Mia and Mom took iced teas to a table on Buccaneer's Island. Their table had a view of High Jinks on the High Seas. It was 11:45, so they had a little longer before it was time to suit up for the dolphin swim. The High Jinks boats had just gone out, and the person manning the water cannon wasn't nearly as talented as Mom and Dad had been. Still, the pirate boat was losing badly.

"I'm proud of you for including your sisters," Mom said.

"I didn't solve the mystery on my own," Mia said. "I understand now what Maddie meant about us helping solve her mystery. I get it now. I didn't then, because I wished I'd been the one to chase down the thief. I couldn't see straight."

"Jealousy can do that to us," Mom said.

"I'm glad you asked me about my reasons for coming today," Mia said. "Yesterday, I was mostly focused on winning. On solving the mystery. But when I got my reasons straight, it was easier to do the right thing. Like to not interrupt when Gabrielle was asking Jackson what I thought were all the wrong questions—that turned out to be the right questions. How did you know what I was going to do, by the way?"

"I know you, sweet Mia," Mom said, smiling. "I could see the frustration written all over your face."

"It was awesome," Mia said. "It was like being in a courtroom when the lawyer is grilling the witness, and the witness doesn't even realize he's the suspect. Then, *wham*! He's caught." She took a sip of her iced tea, watched a pirate fall into the lagoon and start climbing up a thick rope, and then frowned. "What do you think will happen to Jackson?"

"I don't know what level of crime it's considered to let animals out of their habitats," Mom said. "There will definitely be consequences, probably official ones with the park. And it sounded like there would be more at home with his dad."

"He seemed so sure he was doing the right thing, even when what he was doing was so wrong."

"The wrong thing for the right reasons?" Mom asked.

"I still feel mixed up," Mia said. "Last night, you said that sometimes it's just hard to know the right thing to do."

"True," Mom said. "I wish I could tell you that life came with an instruction manual that was simple to follow. But the best instruction manual we have is the Bible."

"Not simple," Mia said.

"No. Sometimes I imagine what it would have been like to be a person sitting on a hillside, listening to Jesus tell stories. All your life you might have thought that faith was cut and dried. The Pharisees certainly made things out to be that way. But along came Jesus, teaching faith with stories that left room for interpretation. And he refused to explain himself or answer all the questions."

"Yeah. Why did he do that?"

"No one knows for sure," Mom said. "But I know that stories are like songs in some ways. The experience of listening to either touches each heart in a unique way. I'm not saying that one thing is true for me and another is true for you. Still, there are layers of meaning in any song or story and in most situations."

"I don't like layers of meaning," Mia said. "I want to know things for sure."

Mom burst out laughing at this. "I know you do."

"What's so funny?" Mia asked.

"It's just that so many people in the world would agree with you. You're right. It would be so much easier if there were black-and-white answers to every question."

"Do you think God wants us to be confused?" Mia asked.

"No. I'm sure he doesn't." Mom stirred the last bit of iced tea in her glass. "I think it all comes down to our hearts."

"Like doing things for the right or wrong reasons?" Mia asked.

"Yes. Sometimes it's hard to even know our own reasons for doing things. We definitely can't be sure of the reasons for other people's choices. God sees

everything, how we're each growing and develop-
ing, how our choices affect the people around us. He
sees every human's life and purpose and the complex
connections that weave us all together. From his perspective, right and wrong are simple to see. But from
our limited perspective, it's not simple at all."

"So that's why we pray?"

"Exactly," Mom said.

"Can we pray for Jackson?" Mia asked.

Mom reached out her hands and took Mia's. "Let's
do that."

"God," Mia prayed. "Please help Jackson. I know
he's in a lot of trouble right now, but I also know he
wanted to do the right thing. He wants the animals to
have exactly what they need, just like I do. Help him to
find the way he can help, a safe way. Oh, and help me
to find a way to fix things with Maddie." She opened
an eye to see if Mom had looked up. Nope. "In Jesus'
name, Amen."

"Amen." Mom took a last sip of her iced tea. "Are
you done with your tea?" Mia handed over her glass
and Mom took both over to the trash bin. "So, needing
to fix things with Maddie?" Mom asked. "Want to talk
about that?"

Mia looked down at her hands. "It's just . . . ever
since London, she's different. I know you said she's
more courageous. I know I should be happy for her. I
suppose I am happy that she's starting to get excited

about singing in your concert. But we used to be so close that we could almost hear one another's thoughts."

"And now you're not?"

"No." Mia hated admitting this out loud. "I'm afraid it will never be like it was. I don't know how to fix it."

"I've never had a twin sister, and I know that makes your relationship with Maddie particularly special. But, I also know that when I was ten and eleven and twelve, I changed too. I started to carve out my own special space in my family. I see you and Maddie doing that. But no matter what changes, you'll always be Glimmer girls. That will always, always be true."

Mia finally looked up, into Mom's eyes. "So I should try to figure out how to be now, rather than try to make things the way they used to be?"

"Sounds like a starting place to me. Relationships aren't very black and white either, are they?"

Mia smiled a watery smile. "No."

Mom checked her phone. "Looks like everyone is here. Are you ready?"

As she stood, Mia's heart beat faster. It was time to talk to Maddie, to tell her sisters about the mystery, and then, finally, to swim with her dolphin. Yes, after the long wait, she was ready.

THIRTY-THREE

Inever get to do the fun stuff!" Lulu shouted as she ran through the gates to see Mia. "You found Dr. Dolittle?"

"Actually, you found him," Mia said. "If you hadn't asked him what he was drawing in his notebook, and he hadn't been so secretive, I never would have put it all together."

Lulu beamed. "I helped!"

Mia gave her a giant hug. "You did."

Maddie hung back, watching. She looked happy, the way she always did when Mia and Lulu worked things out on their own.

"So tell us the story," Dad insisted.

Mia started from when they entered the park, explaining how they'd finally spotted Jackson near the dolphin and seal hospital with the key card, how they'd made their way to Gabrielle's office, and how Gabrielle had tricked him into admitting the truth.

"I asked if they'd let you both swim with the dolphins too. They said it would be too much to have all three of us in the water," Mia said. "I'm sorry."

"You're the one who wanted to swim with them most," Maddie said. "But thank you for asking."

"They said we could all come and watch," Mom said. "And we should hurry, because the appointment is in about fifteen minutes."

"Let me take a quick picture of our detectives," Miss Julia said, snapping a photo.

"Glimmer girls to the rescue again!" Lulu said. "Can that be the caption, Miss Julia?"

"That can absolutely be the caption," she said.

As they walked across the park, Dad put an arm around Mia. "I'm proud of you, Mia. Your dolphins will be safe now, and so will all the other animals."

Zarin met them at the entrance to the dolphin and seal hospital, already in her swimsuit and cap. She had wrapped a towel around her body. "So, Mia, it's time for you to have that swim with the dolphins. Did you wear your swimsuit?"

"We bought one," Mom said.

"You can change in our staff locker room," Zarin said, leading the way. "After you change, you'll want to rinse off and wet your hair. I have a swim cap for you to wear. The rinse and the cap will help protect the dolphins from any lotions or oils on your skin and hair. Plus, the salt water helps too."

"Can Maddie come with me?" Mia asked, needing a little time alone with her sister.

"Of course," Zarin said.

"What about me?" Lulu asked, but Mom swept her toward the windows that faced the sea pens. "While we wait, let's see if we can spot the baby dolphin. Okay?"

"Okay . . ." Lulu said.

Mia and Maddie found a bench, and Mia sat to take off her shoes. With one shoe off, she looked up at Maddie. "I'm sorry, Maddie."

Usually Maddie would ask, "For what?" but she didn't now. Clearly, she knew, just as much as Mia did, that things were off between them.

"Since you snuck out back in London, everything has felt weird. Wrong."

"I tried to apologize," Maddie said.

"No, I'm not blaming you," Mia said. "I know you're sorry for breaking the rules. I accused you of becoming the kind of person who breaks rules, but that wasn't what I meant. I think I was . . . what I was trying to say was . . . I miss you."

"I miss you too," Maddie said. "And I'm sorry for getting upset with you about the treasure hunt. I don't think I was angry about the golden key at all. I think it was just . . ."

"Everything felt wrong," Mia finished her sentence for her. Their eyes caught, and they broke into twin smiles.

Maddie threw her arms around Mia in a giant hug. "Okay, now change already. The dolphins are waiting!"

Mia slipped into her swimsuit and went to rinse off. Maddie helped her into the swim cap, and then they hurried back out to where everyone was waiting.

"I saw the baby dolphin jump!" Lulu announced.

"Awesome!" Maddie and Mia said in unison.

Mom flashed them a bright smile; her girls, back together again. Happiness ballooned in Mia's chest for the second time that day, and then the fizz of excitement grew, too, as they went through the door out onto the dolphin deck.

"Here's a life jacket," Zarin said, handing one over. Mia was a strong swimmer, but the water was deep, she knew, and she didn't want to have to think about anything but the dolphins. She strapped on the jacket. Miss Julia snapped pictures as Mia and Zarin sat on the deck and then slipped into the water. The day had warmed up, so even though the water was cool, it wasn't too much of a shock.

"Come out away from the deck," Zarin urged.

Mia pushed her arms and legs through the water, but then froze as two fins sped toward her, sleek and glistening in the sun.

The dolphins broke apart just before colliding with Zarin and Mia and circling them. Then, one of the dolphins broke out of the circle and nudged Zarin with her snout. Without warning, she flipped over and slapped the water with her tail, dousing both Zarin and Mia with water.

Zarin bobbed underwater and back up again. "Xena's the jokester of the two."

Something smooth and cool slid against Mia's skin. She spun to find herself nose to nose with the other dolphin, Titania. One second, two, three, they stared into one another's faces.

Can you hear me now, now that I'm in the water with you? Mia thought in her direction.

Titania turned away, circled again, and then leapt out of the water in a perfect arc right over the top of Zarin and Mia's heads. She landed on their other side with hardly any splash at all.

Yes. Mia felt the jump had been Titania's answer, though she couldn't know for sure. She wished now she'd asked a more interesting question, something other than "Can you hear me now?" She watched in delight as the dolphins continued to bob and leap through the water. What would the just-right question be?

The two dolphins sped away toward the rock wall. Then, they circled around and swam straight toward Zarin and Mia again. This time they leaped together over their heads, landing together in perfect sync. Joy radiated off the dolphins, shimmering through the air, causing everyone on the deck to break out in applause. Her family's happiness beat in time with Mia's heart. Maybe finding the exact-right question wasn't the point. Whatever the question, the answer was joy. Sunlight danced on the rippling waves as the dolphins approached for another jump. Yes, today, right here in this moment, the answer was joy.

London Art Chase

By Award-Winning Recording Artist Natalie Grant

In *London Art Chase*, the first title in the new Faithgirlz Glimmer Girls series, readers meet 10-year-old twins Mia and Maddie and their adorable little sister, Lulu. All the girls are smart, sassy, and unique in their own way, each with a special little something that adds to great family adventures.

There is pure excitement in the family as the group heads to London for the first time to watch mom, famous singer Gloria Glimmer, perform. But on a day trip to the National Gallery, Maddie witnesses what she believes to be an art theft and takes her sisters and their beloved and wacky nanny, Miss Julia, on a wild and crazy adventure as they follow the supposed thief to his lair. Will the Glimmer Girls save the day? And will Maddie find what makes her shine?

Available in stores and online!